THE NEW JOB

"Sam says you're not supposed to dive without a tender. You're not going to do that, are you?"

"You be my tender," he says suddenly, laying down his knife, leaning on his palms flat on the counter, looking at her through narrowed eyes.

"Me?"

"Why not? You're a big girl. And besides, you owe me."

Without realizing, she'd been tensed up inside, waiting. She knew he'd say something about the money, sooner or later.

"I'm going to get a job," she says. "Don't worry. I'll pay you back."

"You've got a job," he says, with an almost-grin, a challenge in his dark eyes. The abalone in the pan begins to sizzle and he flips it.

"But I don't know how to . . . do whatever it is they do!"

"Tend," he says. "They tend. I'll teach you, don't worry. You can't be any worse than the other morons."

≈≈≈

★ "Haven't we read this one before? A resentful teen, through some fluke of fortune, is forced to reconnect with a long-lost parent. . . . The author's mission is simply (and dauntingly) to present fresh, believable situations that facilitate the inevitable reconciliation and to fashion characters with, well, character, worthy of our caring. In *Tender*, Hobbs not only fulfills but exceeds the goal, creating in the Tragers a fractured family that we'd give our eye teeth to see healthy and healed." —*BCCB*, starred featured review

"Hobbs's storytelling pace [draws] readers in immediately and inextricably. Each character becomes a person whom teens will understand, whether with sympathy or hesitation." —*SLJ*

OTHER BOOKS YOU MAY ENJOY

TENDER

tender

VALERIE HOBBS

PUFFIN BOOKS

PUFFIN BOOKS
Published by Penguin Group
Penguin Young Readers Group, 345 Hudson Street, New York, New York 10014, U.S.A.
Penguin Books Ltd, 80 Strand, London WC2R ORL, England
Penguin Books Australia Ltd, 250 Camberwell Road, Camberwell, Victoria 3124, Australia
Penguin Books Canada Ltd, 10 Alcorn Avenue, Toronto, Ontario, Canada M4V 3B2
Penguin Books (N.Z.) Ltd, 182-190 Wairau Road, Auckland 10, New Zealand

First published in the United States of America by Farrar, Straus and Giroux, 2001
Published by Puffin Books, a division of Penguin Young Readers Group, 2004

10 9 8 7 6 5 4 3 2 1

LIBRARY OF CONGRESS CATALOGING-IN-PUBLICATION DATA
Hobbs, Valerie.
Tender / Valerie Hobbs.
p. cm.
Summary: After her beloved Gran dies, fifteen-year-old Liv goes to California
to live with the father she has never known and must adjust to his gruff ways
and his life as an abalone diver, so different from her life in New York City.
ISBN 0-14-240075-0
[1. Fathers and daughters – Fiction. 2. Deep diving – Fiction. 3. California – Fiction.] I. Title.
PZ7.H65237Te 2004 [Fic]—dc22 2003058592

Printed in the United States of America

FOR FRANCES

ACKNOWLEDGMENTS

The author is indebted to the following members
of her writing groups, whose keen eyes and
generous hearts helped shape *Tender*:
Ellen, Hope, Judy, Lee, Lisa, Marni, and Mary.
Also Dean, Grace, James, Jean, Jennifer, Judy, and Mashey.
A special thanks to Gary Johnson,
abalone and urchin diver, Santa Barbara, California.

TENDER

1

A QUIET MORNING. Only the thin wail of a siren off in the distance. Liv in a tangle of underwear and damp, rumpled sheets. Middle of June, and already the thick heat of summer has settled over the city like an unwelcome blanket.

She gets up, steps over yesterday's clothes. The hallway is cool, cool polished wood on the soles of her bare feet. It won't be cool for long.

In the living room Gran has drawn the shades and set up all four portable fans. They perch precariously on chairs and piles of books, their motors whirring and whining. Gran won't have air conditioning. "Gran?"

No answer.

Back to her room to pull on jeans and a shirt, then out the front door, down the outside hallway with its threadbare ghost-flower carpet. The door to the roof opens with a sulky creak. "Gran?" Her voice tunneling up the narrow stairway.

"Up here, darling!"

Gran kneeling at the side of the flower box. She's wearing her raggedy straw hat, the Hermès scarf Liv gave her for Christmas anchoring the brim flat against her face. Gran doesn't know Hermès from Penney's. She looks up, her face caught between a smile and a frown. "Slugs! How do slugs get all the way up to the roof, I ask you!"

"Don't know, Gran. Do they have wings?"

"Sweetie, look," says Gran, a small armored bug curled on her palm. "Roly-polies. You remember. You used to play with them."

"Yuck."

"Yuck indeed! They're eating their way through our tomatoes." She pulls herself up slowly, brushes dirt from the knees of her baggy jeans. "Like Sherman through Atlanta!"

"Like what?"

"Whom, darling. Like *whom*. General Sherman. Civil War."

"Oh," says Liv, "*that* Sherman." But she really doesn't remember much about the Civil War, which happened more or less last year in American History.

Gran stretches her thin arms wide to take in the entire city. She says what she usually says, no matter the weather. "Isn't it a grand Monday morning, though!" From the roof they can see all the way to the Triborough Bridge, building after building after building. And a patch of almost blue sky.

"Hot," sulks Liv. "School will be un*bear*able!"

Gran sighs dramatically. "And not a fan in the whole

place, I suppose. Certainly not air conditioning. Emma Woods has air conditioning, you know."

"Oh, Gran, give it up. No way would I go back to that boring school!"

"Well, of course not." Up goes Gran's sharp chin. "I know that. I was only saying—" She pretends to be offended, but Liv knows she's not. "Come. I'll make you your oatmeal."

They go down the worn wooden steps, back into the flat. It's too hot for oatmeal, they both know that. But Liv has had oatmeal every morning for as long as she can remember. That's the way it's always been. Oatmeal with raisins and brown sugar, cream drizzled around the outside edge to make an island in the middle.

Well, the island thing is from her childhood, but it's the way she still sees it.

Gran removes her scarf and hat, hangs them together on a hook by the door. She turns and the silk scarf slides in a soft turquoise heap onto the floor.

On the tiny round table with its blue checkered tablecloth there's an article torn from a magazine. Liv picks it up, reads the title aloud: "The Mozart-Math Connection."

There's always *something*.

Gran at the sink, water trickling into the oatmeal pot. "It's the most interesting thing, Liv! They've found that listening to classical music, Baroque especially, affects the brain somehow and"—she turns from the sink to the stove—"*voilà!*"—she waves her wooden spoon, flecks of oatmeal flying—"children magically get better with their numbers. Isn't that something?"

"I'm not flunking math, Gran." Liv lifts the corner of the shade, peers down onto the street, where a man layered in rags is poking through a trashcan. "And I'm not a child."

"Did I *say* you were flunking math?" Gran's sharp gray eyes, wide with feigned innocence.

"No, Gran," Liv sighs, knowing she can't win, "you don't have to *say* anything, you just give me this"—she waves the Mozart article—"all this stupid stuff to read!"

"Oh dear," Gran mutters. Her back is turned, but Liv knows without actually seeing that there's this little cat's grin on Gran's face. "I was so certain you'd be fascinated!" She brings Liv her oatmeal. Liv drizzles on the cream, pokes the raisin people into their places.

The teakettle shrieks and Gran pours water into the Wedgwood teapot, the only piece of her set that she uses for everyday. She carries the pot to the table and returns to the stove. Liv settles the tea cozy over the pot because Gran has forgotten. This worries Liv. Gran is not old, definitely not old. She's not supposed to forget things she does every day of her life. Just last week, for instance, she forgot her hair appointment and had to reschedule with someone she didn't know. Now she has a permanent wave that she hates.

It *is* pretty bad, sort of like a messy bird's nest.

"I've been musing about the summer," says Gran, pulling out the chair opposite Liv at the table and settling into it.

"What do you think? Hal's cottage on the island, or shall we take one of those tours somewhere? We haven't decided, you know."

Swirling her spoon through the cream, making rivers. "I know . . ."

"Uncle" Hal. Liv has known him all her life, but he's Gran's best friend.

Gran says nothing more, just studies Liv openly, as if her granddaughter is a source of continual fascination. People say all the time that Gran is beautiful, not beautiful for a sixty-seven-year-old lady, just beautiful period. Mostly it's her brilliant gray eyes. Everything she's feeling, you can see right there. "Have you gotten too big to travel with your old grandmother?" she says, humor and just a touch of sadness in her voice. "Am I boring now?" She tries to say "boring" the way Liv does, "*bO*-ring!" which makes Liv giggle.

It's true. Going on vacation with Gran *is* boring. And it's not just Gran. At Hal's all they do is play cribbage. If Liv goes to the beach, which she does every day that they're on the island, she's alone. And a tour? Gran means one of those old-lady things. "You're not boring, Gran," she says, but she won't look up, because Gran reads eyes the way a fortune-teller reads palms.

"Your father sent some money," Gran says quietly.

Liv looks up. "Yeah?"

"Four hundred dollars. Quite a surprise!" Gran sips her tea, frowning over the steam rising from the cup.

"Did he, like, send, you know, anything else?" The words hurt to say, each one, a separate little stab.

"A letter you mean? Now *that* would be a surprise, wouldn't it?" Her voice intentionally light, she cups Liv's hand, giving it a quick squeeze. "I'm sorry, darling. Your father isn't what one might call communicative, is he?"

"No shit!"

A real frown now. "Must you, Olivia?"

"Well, *Gran*! How do you expect me to feel? He doesn't even send *birthday* cards! *Christmas* presents! Just a couple of hundred bucks whenever he feels like it!" Her appetite drowned in the swamp of her anger, Liv pushes away her oatmeal, slumps down in her chair with crossed arms.

Gran's softly lined face, so sad. Liv looks away, blinking back tears. Why tears? It's been fifteen years, all her life, always the same. Why does she keep expecting something more from him? She looks back at Gran, sees that Gran is fixing her a cup of tea, though she seldom drinks it now, only coffee, black coffee. A whopping spoonful of sugar goes into the tea already laced with milk. "There," Gran says, "nothing like a cup of tea to brighten the day. Right, my girl?"

"Oh, Gran," groans Liv, but she has to smile. Gran's eyes won't allow anything else, and with the smile her mood lifts. There's only a week left of school. She and Suds and Megan with a whole summer of nothing to do but hang out. But she will spend some time with Gran, too. Mostly because Gran needs her to. "Maybe we could go to, like,

Bermuda!" she offers. "Or Hawaii! Just us. Not with a bunch of people. How about that?"

"Well," Gran hesitates, thinking it through. "I suppose we *could* do something a little different. Something exotic!" She wriggles her eyebrows. "Ooh-la-la, huh?"

Liv cracks up. "*Ooh-la-la?*"

"It's an old saying. Don't worry about it. You're too young for ooh-la-la, anyway."

"Oh, yeah?"

"Yeah."

"Oh, yeah?"

"Yeah!"

Gran gives in first. "You'd better get ready for school." She squints at the dainty silver watch on her thin wrist. "It's seven-twenty. By the time you put on all that black makeup, you'll be late."

"Don't start, Gran!" Liv warns. She gets up, rinses out her oatmeal bowl, and sets it in the sink.

"Me? Heaven forbid. No, no. I *want* you to wear your makeup. Every bit of it."

"*Sure* you do!"

"Liv, darling. I do! Believe me, I know what would happen if you didn't hide behind all that stuff."

"I'm not hiding, Gran." Fists on her hips, she glares down at her grandmother, who's a foot shorter than she.

"No, of course you're not. You wear it because . . . because . . ." Gran pretends to be looking hard for an answer on the ceiling.

"Because it's *in*. Because it's *cool*! Oh, Gran, forget it." Liv's hands go up, then drop. "You wouldn't understand."

"No," sighs Gran, feigning hurt feelings again, "I never do. I try, but I just never do." She follows Liv down the hall, chuckling softly. She stops outside the bathroom as Liv goes in.

It's too late for a shower. Liv gives her teeth a quick brush, spits, and wipes her mouth. "What did you mean you 'know what would happen . . .'?"

"If you didn't wear your makeup?"

"Yeah."

"Oh, sweetie, you don't want to know."

"I do!" Gran's sucking her in, she can feel it. But she always plays along, because Gran's such a crack-up.

"Well, we'd have to hire a bodyguard, darling. And we can't afford one."

"A bodyguard?"

"Well, yes. How else would we protect you from all the young men who would be hanging about? following you home? climbing the fire escape!"

"Oh, *right*!"

Gran's look turns serious and thoughtful. "I'm not entirely fooling, you know. You *are* a beautiful girl, Olivia Trager."

"Oh, Gran, I'm not either. I'm not even pretty." Liv frowns at her plain brown eyes, the straight-as-a-stick eyebrows that make her look so serious even when she's not, her pale unmade-up face. Around it, the spikes of her dyed black hair with the latest addition: tangerine tips. Like flames. They were supposed to look like flames, but they don't. She reaches for her kohl pencil and begins, with a steady, careful hand, to line her eyes top and bottom with a thick black line. Blackest Beauty is the name of her new lipstick. She can't wait to put it on. By the time she applies the third coat of mascara, she'll be late. Again.

Behind her in the mirror: Gran's tiny narrow face, her amused silvery gray eyes.

2

TUESDAY. MIDDLE OF FOURTH PERIOD. Yellow slip from the office.

Liv looks up. So do Suds and a couple of other kids. Idly, their minds on the poetry project. Their eyes on the poetry project, their minds on other things. Mr. Denker frowns at the yellow slip, looks out over his glasses. "Olivia, it's for you."

Suds looks surprised. Liv shrugs. It's about being late so often, but she can deal with that. She gets up, weaves her way through the clustered desks to the front of the room. Watches the yellow note get folded into Mr. Denker's palm. Sees his eyes get wide and sad-looking. "Your grandmother is in the hospital, Olivia," he says, almost under his breath, his eyes shifting to the other kids and back to her. "Mercy Hospital. Can you get there on your own, or do you need someone to take you?"

Mr. Denker with his wire-rimmed glasses and frizzy gray

hair looks like someone she's never seen before. His face wobbles and she blinks. Gran? How could Gran be in the hospital? This morning in her kitchen humming a Beatles tune, making Liv's oatmeal.

"Um, I can get there," she says, suddenly breathless, and her mind makes the moves ahead: six blocks to the subway, then a bus across town. In her purse, a couple of dollars, not much more.

"Are you sure?" He wants to help. He wants to get back to the poetry. Both at once.

Liv likes Mr. Denker. He gets lost in poetry, and so does she sometimes. He doesn't put you down for being alternative.

"Um, if you could loan me some money for a cab—"

"Of course! Of course!" Relieved. Something he can do now. Going right into action, stuffing both hands into his pockets and coming out empty. "My wallet! In my brief-case!" Shuffling through that, finding a shabby cloth wallet out of which, like a magician pulling a rabbit, he extracts a limp ten-dollar bill.

She wants to cry. So scared, and there is Mr. Denker with his ten-dollar bill and his shy, worried smile. "Thanks!" she says. Can't look at him anymore. Doesn't dare look at anyone in the class, too many watching, wondering. Everybody dreads the note from the office, and this is the worst kind.

Down the hallway, her boots echoing the emptiness, the bank of graffiti-covered lockers no longer used. Too many drugs, too many guns.

She will get there in time and Gran will be all right. They will say that it's her heart. She has to take it easier. She won't, and that is the trouble. She wants to live a normal life. As long as she can, she says.

It isn't fair. Gran is all Liv has.

Outside, the heat hits like a moving wall, only she is the one moving. Moving through it, running, headed for Tenth Avenue, where she can find a cab. Not here, not at a New York City public high school. You will never find a taxi here. Prison zone.

Two years it took to talk Gran into letting her go to public school. She'd had to make a lot of promises. Most of them she's kept.

She will keep the rest, every one, if only Gran is all right.

Wrong day for the leather jacket, but she keeps it on anyway, sweating inside it, thinking if she suffers enough then God will feel sorry. If there is a God, which she isn't so sure of. Out of breath, running for Tenth.

And God is there on the corner, a dark little guy—she can hardly understand him—in a yellow taxi. "Mercy Hospital," she says, sliding across the torn back seat.

"Merky wha'?" His eyes crazy in the rearview mirror.

She says the name of the hospital again, slowly and clearly, her fingers like claws on the back of his seat, and he tears off up Tenth, seeming to understand.

Ahmed Muzhaki, his name is. You never know if the license is for real or not. There was that serial rapist who drove a taxi for a living, everybody knew about it. Took girls like her all the way out to Westchester, raped them, gave them a rose, and then drove them all the way back again. Like some weirdo's idea of a date.

Gran gets a checkup every six months. Has to. She comes from a long line of bad hearts, she says. It's a joke, sort of. Her father left his wife, Liv's great-grandmother, in the middle of a Minnesota blizzard when she was about to deliver their sixth child. Gran's uncles were drunks, and her brothers weren't much better. They'd just as soon skin a live cat than chop firewood. Bad hearts every one.

The women held things together. Good women with faulty heart valves.

Liv's mother for one. Liv had only minutes with her, maybe less, as the last breath left her and Liv took her first. Liv doesn't remember this, of course, but she knows the story like a prayer.

Just Gran and Liv ever since.

The taxi careens around a bus, stops too quickly at the light. A screech of brakes behind, a horn blares. The driver yells something in his own language. A curse, the same sound in any country.

Mercy looms up from the street like a wall of gray water, a tidal wave cresting. She pays the driver, runs for the stone steps.

Emergency. Emergency. Somewhere down a hamster maze of hallways. They've got her grandmother there. She races down a narrow corridor to a set of double doors. AUTHORIZED PERSONNEL ONLY. DO NOT ENTER. Back down the hall. No signs anywhere. She guesses again, this time correctly.

Out of breath, she stops the first person wearing green, the color of emergency.

"Yes, she's here," the nurse says. Taller than Liv, which is tall. Chapped lips, burning candle eyes. "I'll let you know if you can see her." Rosa, her name badge says.

If? "Is she all right? Is my Gran all right?"

How can somebody dressed like this, all leather and chains, have such a nice little grandmother, the nurse Rosa thinks. Liv can see this in the candle eyes.

"Your grandmother has had a heart attack," the nurse says carefully, softly, as if Liv could blow like a homemade bomb. "We've got her stabilized. She's in CCU. The waiting room is just down this hall." She turns Liv by the shoulder, a gentle turning. "Wait there," she says.

The room is full. It's full of people Liv doesn't want to know. And kids, little kids.

She waits in the hall, slumping down to the floor, her long legs out where people have to step over them. She hardly realizes this.

Stabilized. CCU. But what does that *mean*?

She hadn't smoked all the way over. For Gran. And besides, she's run out of cigarettes. But now she needs one—who wouldn't? She folds up her long legs, gets to her feet.

Outside the glass door, next to an ambulance, three guys in blue uniforms, one of them smoking. Liv bums a cigarette. Not a second look at her spiked hair, her leather and chains, from the guy who gives it to her. Seen it all, he has. And worse, too.

Everybody sweating. Sweaty armpits, foreheads. Like fish in a sewer; people weren't meant to live in Manhattan in the summer.

So maybe she and Gran will go to Fire Island in July, stay with Gran's gay friend, Hal. Gay is all right. Part of God's rainbow. She learned that from Gran when she was very young. Everything from Gran.

What a talker Gran is. All these old sayings. Stuff like getting tougher when the going gets tough, making lemonade when life hands you lemons. Gran tries to build a kind of word-house around Liv with those sayings. A shelter to curl up inside when the storms come on. If Liv ever lost her Gran, she'd be on her own.

Well, she'd have her father. Liv drops the cigarette, stubs it out with the toe of her boot. She'd have her father. Which is just another way of saying the same thing. She'd have nobody.

The guys jump into the ambulance, all three at once. Doors slam, the siren screams. Light swirling, they swoop out into the traffic that stops like a held breath. Even in New York.

3

OUTSIDE THE SLIDING GLASS DOOR, EMERGENCY in bright red letters overhead, Liv paces until she can barely breathe from the heat. She goes back inside. Not yet, the nurse Rosa says, busy with other things, other people, other grandmothers.

Liv digs into her pocket for change. She waits by the telephone for the guy who's had a baby, whose wife had a baby. He's telling somebody about it, holding the receiver in his left hand, his right hand massaging his forehead. He could be talking about death is how he looks.

She dials Suds's number. The ringing goes on forever, no answering machine at the Molina house, no TV either. Hard to believe, but true. She hangs up the phone.

The waiting room is empty. Plastic furniture pea green, so ugly you can taste it in the back of your throat. Magazines with beat-up covers. Liv sits on the edge of the couch. Drained inside, nothing inside but fear. She doesn't know her eyes are closed until she hears her name.

It's the nurse. Rosa the nurse. She looks angry. But she's not; that's just how she looks. "I'm sorry," she says, "did you tell me your name?"

Liv tells her again. Or she tells her the first time, she doesn't remember.

"I'm sorry, Liv," she says again, "but your grandmother has passed."

Passed out? Passed the exam? "What?" Liv yells this, loud. Louder than she, than anybody, is supposed to.

The nurse touches her hand. "She went into cardiac arrest," she says. "They couldn't pull her through." She waits, her dark eyes burning.

Is that brown stain on her sleeve blood? Liv is supposed to understand something, make Rosa the nurse feel not so sorry, not so bad. For some reason she doesn't know, Liv plasters both her hands over her mouth. She hears herself making these funny little animal noises behind her hands. Huff, huff, huff. It's that or scream.

"Do you want to see her?"

See her?

"Say goodbye?"

Liv nods. She doesn't know if this is something she can do. See a person dead. But what if it's all a mistake? Maybe if she's in the room, Gran will come back. They do that sometimes, she's heard somewhere. They do that if they're really needed. They come back when there's somebody who can't go on without them, like their kid.

"Is there somebody I can call?" the nurse asks. "Your mother?"

Liv shakes her head.

"Nobody?" The nurse doesn't look as if she believes this, but what can she do?

Liv stumbles up off the couch, follows the green back of the nurse past sick people lined up in the hallways on gurneys. A special kind of doctor works on them right there, in the hallway. Like they're all on an assembly line in a factory. A factory doctor. She giggles with an edge of hysteria.

The nurse turns, gives her a knowing look. She knows what death does to the person not dying. This she has seen.

CARDIAC CARE UNIT say the white letters on the black plastic sign. CCU. Rosa touches the door. "Do you want me to come in with you?"

It's the kindness that's the worst, like Mr. Denker's, because then she'll break down and never get up again.

"Nuh-uh," she says. Then, "No, thank you," because of Gran, because on the other side of this door, Gran might hear.

The door opens. Liv's hand is on the doorknob, holding on to it. She steps inside the room. It is dark, dark with the buzz of machines and green lights blinking. A nurse looks up from a clipboard she is writing on. "Are you a relative?"

Liv nods.

The nurse, this one young, seems to read something in Liv's eyes. "I'll leave you alone with her," she says. "If you need me, I'll be next door."

Liv stands in the semidarkness, her eyes like an animal's, adjusting to the cave. Across the room the person that is supposed to be her grandmother, a small form under a white sheet. Except that it's her real face, her pointy nose, and so it must be her. Closer, there's no mistaking it. The bird's-nest perm. Gran without her glasses, as if she's just closed her eyes for a nap.

Liv breathes. She has to remind herself to breathe just like always, in and out.

Gran's arms at her sides against the white, white sheet. Her left hand with the thinnest gold wedding band. From Grandpa, the hero Liv never knew, standing by the jet fighter. *For my love,* says the picture on Gran's nightstand.

There's a feeling in this room Liv has never felt before. Stillness, but more than that. Deeper. After this she will know what stillness really is. She will always know.

"Gran?" Her voice timid, embarrassed. How can she be so stupid? Nobody's here. Nobody can hear her talking to a . . . to a person who's supposed to be dead. "Gran?" Louder this time, and the tears gush out, unstoppable, unpluggable. "Gran? Come *on,* Gran!" She shakes Gran's arm, a nudge, that's all, as if it's Christmas morning and Gran has to get up. As if Liv is seven years old again and she's already seen that there's a Barbie in a Barbie house under the tree, even though Gran had said there'd never be a Barbie in this house, never.

Stillness. This is what it means when the spirit is gone. There's this stillness left behind. Gran isn't coming back. She can't, her spirit's gone.

Still holding on to her grandmother, Liv sinks to the

floor by the side of the bed. She lays her face against the white sheets and sobs like the seven-year-old she still is, will probably always be without her Gran.

The door creaks behind her. Liv lifts her head. Streaks of black mascara across the white sheets. She makes herself get up. Light from the door floods across Gran, but Gran doesn't see it.

Rosa is next to her, an arm around Liv's back, the other hand patting Liv's left shoulder. "Let's go, okay? We'll find somebody to call."

Liv lets herself be led from the room. "Wait!" she cries, at the door, before it's too late. She pulls from the nurse's hold on her and hurries back to Gran. What would they do if she just climbed into that bed? If she curled up right next to Gran? Would they think she was a freak? Would they send her to the psych ward? She bends over, touches Gran's forehead with her lips. Feels like crying all over again because of the permanent. She can smell it in Gran's frizzy hair. Gran would be so mad if she knew. But then she would laugh. At herself, for making such a fuss over nothing.

"I love you, Gran," she whispers, through glass shards in her throat.

Rosa, the nurse angel, waits at the door.

4

"OLIVIA? OLIVIA TRAGER?" Kinky orange hair, rhinestone-studded cat-eye sunglasses, cut-off jeans above bony, freckled knees and rubber thongs. "I'm Samantha— Sam. A friend of your father's." She sticks out a strong, freckle-spotted hand.

Liv shakes it, dazed. From the time she boarded the plane at Kennedy, changed planes in Denver, until now, getting ready for her father, arming herself like a soldier heading into war. And now this instead. "Where's my father?"

"Disappointed, aren't you?" A sigh. "Well, I told him you would be. It's the weather," she says, as if that explains things.

Liv follows the woman who calls herself Sam past a wall of bright purple flowers to a sort of outdoor tent where the bags are being unloaded. "Weather?"

"Yeah. You'll have to get used to it, I'm afraid. Your dad's out there"—she nods her curly head in what Liv assumes is the direction of the Pacific Ocean—"diving. Every chance he gets. Which means every day the weather's good." Sam scans the rack of suitcases. "Which are yours?"

Liv pulls her biggest suitcase off the rack. "That one, too," she says, and Sam grabs the smaller bag. It is heavier than it looks, filled with her music and her stereo. Without her music she will not survive this. *With* it, she might not survive this.

"I told your dad I'd get you settled. I think he's a little nervous about, well, you know . . . about seeing you after all these years." Sam is a short person, almost a midget if you didn't count the hair. She removes the cat-eye glasses and squints up at Liv with nearsighted green eyes, full of humor and sadness and some craziness, too, maybe.

Like a boxer with a canceled fight, Liv reels from not having to face off with the man who is her father.

"I guess you're a little nervous, too, huh?"

"I guess," Liv says.

They cross the road to the parking lot. Liv's brand-new lizard-skin boots are pinching her toes. She bought the boots the day of her grandmother's funeral with the money Gran left in a dresser drawer in an envelope marked *Vacation*. The boots made her feel a little better. For almost a whole day. She and Gran had talked about all this, about what could happen someday. That she might have to live with her father someday.

Someday, which was never supposed to happen.

It takes both Sam and Liv hauling together to load the

bags into the back of the station wagon, an old green Volvo that looks like the lone survivor of a freeway pileup.

Liv's first real look at California from the window of the Volvo steals the breath right out of her. The median strip on the highway blooms like something out of *The Wizard of Oz*, with Popsicle pink and orange flowers. Palm trees shoot into a baby blue sky and explode there, like fireworks. Convertibles in every shade of Dorothy's rainbow fly past in the fast lane, driven by girls who look like movie stars, the neon yellow flags of their hair flying.

Liv hunkers down in her black leather jacket, fists stuffed in her pockets.

"I'm sorry about your grandmother," Sam says, burrowing around inside a fat straw purse, eyes on the road, steering left-handed. Out comes a half-crushed pack of Pall Malls and an ancient Zippo lighter. "Please say you don't smoke," she says, but chuckles understanding when Liv takes a cigarette.

"Your dad will give you no end of grief about that," she says. "He won't let you smoke inside. Don't you dare tell him I gave you one."

She won't, Liv says.

"He's . . . um . . ." Sam nibbles a fleck of tobacco off her lip and considers. "He's not exactly an easy person to get to know, Liv." She looks at Liv, trying to read her New York face and failing. "I thought I ought to tell you that about him, but I guess you could say it's none of my business . . ."

She waits.

The truth is, Liv wants to know everything, everything Sam can tell her about the man she's never seen, never even heard from. But she's not about to ask. Sam would think she cares, and she doesn't. How can you care about somebody you don't even know? "Are you his, like, girlfriend or something?"

Half-grin, half-frown. "Yeah, *something*. We don't live together, though. It'll just be you and your dad. His place is pretty small—" She breaks off. "Well, you'll see. Before he knew you were coming, he lived on his boat in the harbor. Then he got the apartment."

They drive straight past the city of Santa Barbara. Pop. 85,000. Cutesy little shops and stuff. What Gran would call "charming." But when they finally get to Carpinteria, where her father lives, Liv's heart bottoms out. There is nothing here at all, not for kids, not for *anybody*. They stop at a traffic light that hangs from a wire strung over the narrow sand-strewn main street. To the left, a single-pump gas station. To the right, a weedy vacant lot. Up ahead, on either side of the road, shacks that are people's actual homes. "Is this *it*?"

Sam doesn't catch the panic in Liv's voice. "This is it!" she trills. "Home sweet home. Sun and sand. Your dad's place is less than half a mile from the beach. You're going to love it here, Liv."

Is the woman totally *out of her mind*?

"I mean, this is the *whole* thing? The whole city?"

Sam pulls into the gravel lot of Hope Apts and Motel

and parks, the old Volvo engine shuddering to a stop. "The whole shootin' match," she says. Her door opens with a metallic yawn. "Come on, let's put your stuff inside and grab a hamburger. I'll bet you're starved. Teenagers are always starving, that's one thing I know."

Hope Apts and Motel is a single row of shabby rooms joined at the hip, with faded blue doors and peeling white siding. A vine with dead, spiny tendrils clings to the roof. At the far end of the parking lot, a car with 23 painted on the side but no wheels is propped up on cinder blocks. Grayish-white towels hang on a sagging line strung from the end of the building to a telephone pole.

Sam fits a key into the lock on the door to Number 5, jiggling until it gives. The door opens and Liv peers in. Brown. Everything is brown. Carpet, drapes, couch, everything. "You're going to have to give it the woman's touch." Sam sighs, hauling a suitcase over the doorsill. Then she chuckles. Liv, standing in the middle of that room dressed in black leather, her hair dyed black and orange, silver chains and ear studs. "Well, you know. Jazz it up a little!"

Sam manages to get both suitcases into the bedroom while Liv stands paralyzed, hardly knowing how to fit this awful place into her life as she knows it. Sagging brown plaid couch and matching brown chair. Tiny little television set with antennae sticking out of the top. Can this be *real*?

Several cardboard boxes are lined under the one window (brown drapes) that looks out onto the parking lot. In the boxes are plaid shirts and jeans neatly folded, several of the grayish-white towels (also folded), a man's blue shaving kit.

She doesn't belong here. She belongs with her Gran. A fierce deep longing for her old life washes through the pit of her stomach. Who knew her like Gran? Who but Gran would have let her be whoever she thought she was all those years—punk rocker, honor student, aspiring model, commercial artist. Gran knew all the Livs the way no one else ever did, or could, because she knew the real one underneath.

No one knows her now.

"I put a few things in here," Sam calls from the bedroom. Like a sleepwalker, Liv follows the sound of her voice. "But you don't have to keep them if you don't want to. They're just until you get your own things. You know . . ."

Sam fusses a little with a pink chenille bedspread, embarrassed. On the dresser a ceramic ballerina with a self-satisfied smug doing a pirouette.

Who were they expecting? Pippi Longstocking?

Liv wants to bolt. She wants to head out the door and run in her black lizard boots straight to the nearest taxi and get the hell out of here. Her chest hurts like she's been punched. "Where's my da . . . Where's *his* room?" she asks.

"Oh, he'll sleep on the couch," Sam says. "He doesn't really need a room. He's used to living on a boat. Which is good, you know. He's neat. I mean, he's a neat *freak*. If I were you, I'd just keep the door to my room shut at all times. Then he can't get on your case."

Shut! She'd put a padlock on it. Outside and inside!

Sam senses the panic Liv can't hide. "Oh, honey, don't worry. Your father's a good man. I would trust him with my life, and have, believe me. He's just, well, kind of gruff at first." She stops, seems to be thinking what to say next. "But he's harmless. The thing is . . . he just doesn't know how to talk to people, how to be, well, *social*. I don't know if he ever did, or if . . . Well, I just don't know. Try and be patient with him if you can. Give him a chance to get to know you. He'll open up after a while."

"Let's get out of here," Liv says, and heads for the door.

Sam hangs back. "You wanna change or anything first?"

"Huh? Oh, yeah, I guess." Liv shucks her leather jacket, stomps back, and tosses it onto the bed.

They walk to the Surf Hut, a ramshackle hamburger stand with a couple of surfboards nailed to one wall and a crude painting of a wave set on another. Liv orders a fish sandwich and picks off all the coating while Sam polishes off a double cheeseburger and a pile of greasy fries. "This is why he came out here, you know," Liv says, nodding at the longboards.

"Your dad?"

"That's what Gran said."

"You mean he came all the way out here just to learn how to surf?"

Liv shrugs. "I guess."

"Oh, sweetie," Sam says, "there had to be more to it." She wipes catsup and lipstick off her lips with a paper napkin and reaches for a cigarette.

"You mean because he abandoned me?"

Sam's hand with the lighter stops short of the cigarette. Her green eyes widen enough to let Liv see the punch of her words, the way she intended them. She isn't about to pretend that her father ever cared at all what became of her. He'd simply passed her over to Gran, like a bundle of dirty clothes for the wash.

"He was a kid, honey," Sam says. "A heartbroken kid."

"Yeah, well," Liv says.

"Whoa," Sam says softly, with a sad slow shake of her head. She blows a plume of smoke upward, her lips puckered and shiny. Then she looks back at Liv with that near-sighted squint. "This isn't going to be so easy, is it?"

"Not if I can help it," Liv says, and reaches for the Pall Malls.

Scuffing along in her rubber thongs, Sam gives Liv the "city tour." They walk in the direction of the beach, Liv's boots hammering the cracked and broken sidewalks. Sand everywhere, drifting like cocoa powder across the narrow main street, caught in the corners of shop windows.

The shops have nothing to do with Liv, with her life. Clementine's Bakery, a bait-and-tackle shop, Carpinteria Hardware, a shop selling old-lady clothes, a Salvation Army thrift store. Shear Magic, the hair salon where Sam works. Liv is tired from the long plane ride and lack of sleep in Suds's lumpy double bed. After Gran . . . well, after Gran *passed away* (she still doesn't know how to say this), Liv went back to the flat only once. Suds went along, holding her hand. In the kitchen, Liv's oatmeal bowl, Gran's Wedgwood teapot, Gran's turquoise scarf and raggedy straw hat hanging on the peg where they belonged. She and Suds whispered, packing Liv's clothes. There was Hal for everything else, for putting stuff in storage and handling the will.

"A little different from New York, huh?"

Liv emerges from her memory fog. "I guess."

"Olivia?" Sam says, an edge to her voice Liv hasn't heard before.

She stops walking because Sam has. Sam stands there, looking up at Liv through those cat-eye glasses, fists on her narrow hips. "Do you *know* anything?"

"Huh?" Off-guard. Gran never let her get away with "Huh?" It was always "Pardon?" or "What did you say?"

"You're always *guessing*! Guess this, guess that . . ." Sam says. "It's hard to know what you think about *anything*."

And so Liv does what she does best: she shuts down. Instead of talking, she grunts replies to whatever she's asked, and after a while Sam stops asking.

"Well, there it is." Sam sighs, and Liv can tell that the whole sun-sparkled green-blue ocean would have been a kind of gift from Sam if Liv had let it be. But by that time they are both in a sulk. Sam has given up on Liv. Liv tells herself she doesn't care.

Slipping off her rubber sandals, Sam walks out onto the sand. Liv watches her go. She stands there on the edge of things, in her black jeans and lizard-skin boots, and watches the woman who has tried to be her friend head for the water with her hands stuffed into the pockets of her faded cutoffs. Gray-and-white birds—seagulls, she guesses—lift up off their stick legs into the air, then settle again after Sam has passed. In the distance, against a low line of islands, a fishing boat plows its way up the coast.

5

SAM COMES BACK through the soft sand, head down, deep in thought, trudging duck-footed through the sand.

"I'll stick around till your dad comes home, Olivia," she says, wary now, looking sideways up at Liv. "If you want me to."

Liv wants her to. She hasn't admitted, even to herself until this minute, how terrified she is, how really freaked she is, about seeing her father. "Yes, please," she says contritely.

Sam checks Liv over for signs of sarcasm, like a doctor scanning for measles. "Okay," she says.

"You can call me Liv," Liv says. *"Please."*

Just before they would have turned the corner to Hope Apts and Motel, Sam says, "Look, Liv." The sky above the sea has sent up a show while their backs were turned, stripes of smoky purple threaded like loose yarn through bands of brilliant orange. As they watch, the sun melts into a thin golden thread and disappears.

"Whoa!" Liv says, in spite of herself.

"Whoa, indeed," laughs Sam, shaking her head and smiling. "Whoa, indeed."

Liv has been given a second chance.

They sip from cans of root beer, sitting in plastic chairs on the narrow cement porch, watching the night set up around them in shadows. Sam has said that "Mark" will be home shortly after dark. Sometimes he hangs out for a while with the other divers and fishermen, swapping sea stories. Sam is sure he won't be doing that tonight, since Liv is here, but it is a long time before Liv hears her say, "That's him now."

A pickup truck clatters to a stop in the vacant lot next to the apartments. Sam gets up, Liv can't. She watches the man who is her father, a dark hulking shape, emerge from the truck, slam the door behind him. Hanging from his right hand is a bucket that sloshes with each heavy step he takes. His face comes clearer in the yellow light of the porch: square jaw, broad forehead with deep vertical lines, thinning hair (this surprises Liv most). He is taller than she thought he would be and heavier, but heavy like a tree trunk, with that solid, immovable kind of density.

"You're home!" Sam cries, her voice cracking like a thirteen-year-old boy's. Sam is nervous, too. Who wouldn't be? It is a momentous occasion, supposed to be, but no one seems to know what to do with it.

"Olivia," says her father. His voice is very deep and he says her name with an unreadable flatness. If her thick black eyeliner and purplish-black lipstick surprise or offend him, he doesn't let on.

"Hello," Liv says.

The space and the silence between them is nothing either can deal with.

"Well!" says Sam, with a bright smile and a clap of her hands, like a magician when the trick hasn't worked. "Let's go inside."

And that is their meeting.

In the kitchen her father puts the plastic bucket in the sink. "Got us some dinner," he says. "You two eat?" He turns from the sink, his eyes skimming past Liv to Sam, anchoring there. His eyes are bloodshot, the flat planes of his face reddened, raw-looking.

"We were waiting for you." Sam never takes her eyes off him as he rummages under the sink and pulls out an electric hot plate. There is puzzlement, or maybe puzzled amusement, in her eyes. She can't believe what Liv can't believe: either her father is pretending that she isn't there, or he has decided to act as if she has never been anywhere else.

Sam fills all the awkward silences. "Look, Liv," she says, leaning over the bucket. Liv peers in, feeling Sam's hand lightly on her back. "That's an abalone. Ever see one before?"

"Looks like a chunk of cement," Liv says. Her father shoots her a look.

"Just wait till you taste it," promises Sam. "If it isn't the best thing you ever ate, I'll owe you a"—she stops to think—"fishburger." Behind Liv's father's back, Sam pretends to be smoking, letting Liv know the real bet is a pack of cigarettes.

"Lots of cement where you come from, isn't that right?" Her father pauses and looks straight at Liv, frowning, his hands with the abalone in them dripping water.

"That's right," Liv says, staring right back.

"Huh," says her father. He puts down a heavy cutting board and takes a huge bone-handled knife from a drawer. Before Liv can see exactly how he does it, he has the abalone out of the shell. It's slimy gray until it's trimmed. Then it looks like a chunk of lard. Sam rinses the big empty shell and lays it in Liv's hands. The lining is a glimmering kaleidoscope of pale pink, green, silver, and turquoise. Liv traces a fingertip over its smooth wet surface.

"Keep it in your room," Sam says, when Liv tries to hand it back.

"That's okay," Liv says, and sets it on the countertop.

"How was the flight?"

"Huh?" She's caught by surprise again. "The flight?"

"The flight from New York," he says. He cuts the naked abalone into half-inch slices, cracks and beats an egg, drags the slices through it. On the hot plate, in a frying pan, butter sizzles.

"Good," Liv says. "Fine. The flight was fine."

"Peanuts?"

"Pardon me?"

"Peanuts. Did they give you peanuts?"

Liv scans his profile for some sign that he's joking, pulling her leg, as Gran used to say. But if he is, she can't tell.

"Pretzels," she says.

"Huh," he says, fussing with the abalone bubbling in the butter.

Liv tries to translate that "huh." It's more air than meaning, a flat grunt.

A loony grin stuck on her face, Sam takes three plates out of the cupboard and sets the table. For napkins, she folds paper towels into hats and sets them on the plates. None of the forks or knives match. Liv notices things like that because of Gran, whose taste is impeccable. Is/was. Gran's china and silver have been placed in storage until Liv either learns to appreciate them or marries. One or the other is supposed to occur in Liv's lifetime.

The abalone is done in minutes, her father flipping the slices when they've barely turned a golden yellow. He brings the slices to the table in the frying pan and forks them onto their plates. "There," he says, "try that."

It is like nothing Liv's ever tasted.

"What did I tell you?" says Sam, her eyes encouraging. Understanding what Liv is going through, but still encouraging.

"Yeah," she says.

"Yeah, what?" Her father's eyes are dark and deep-set. When he looks at you, there is no looking away.

She shrugs. "It's good," she says.

They finish their dinner, such as it is, in silence.

Her father gets up and sets his empty plate on the counter. Then he goes into the other room. The toilet flushes.

Sam tosses Liv a dish towel and begins washing up.

Liv bites her lip, but it slips out anyway: "Can I come and, like, stay with you?"

"Jeez, Liv," Sam says slowly, suds dripping from her hands, "I don't know . . . I don't have much room. And besides, I think your father—"

"Never mind." Liv drops the dish towel on the counter, stalks into the living room. Her father has switched on the television and is working the rabbit's ears, twisting them this way and that to clear the snow from the screen. A cowboy with stones in his mouth is trying to say goodbye to a blonde, the one who went off to become the Princess of Monaco, but the snow keeps blowing in between them. Her father changes the channel to a *Twilight Zone* rerun with better reception. He sits heavily in the scoop of the ugly brown chair, his arms resting on the chair arms, his big square hands dangling.

Liv turns and goes back into the kitchen.

"You want me to ask him?" Sam says quietly, her straw purse tucked under her arm.

"Ask him what?"

"If you can stay with me. You know, for tonight."

"Are you leaving already?"

"I'll ask him if you want me to." She puts a hand on Liv's arm.

"That's okay," Liv says, looking down at the scratched linoleum, a brown-and-tan puzzle.

"Here," she says, using Liv as a shield while she reaches into her purse and extracts two cigarettes. "But not in the house, okay?"

Liv tucks them into her bra.

"Come by and see me tomorrow at work."

Liv watches Sam go into the living room and plop herself down into Mark's lap. A look of amusement crosses his face, a slight fissure in the stone. "I'm heading out, sugar," she says, messing with what's left of his hair. "You going out again in the morning?"

"Got to," he says.

"Can't you take just one day off? Show Liv around? Grace has got the flu, so it's just Helen and me at the shop."

"Can't," he says. "Olivia can come out with me, if she wants . . ."

"Hey, what about that?" Sam hops up out of the lap. Liv is leaning against the open doorway that separates the kitchen from the living room, watching them in the reflected gray light of the television screen. Her father is a little like that dumb cowboy on TV. It makes no sense to her that Sam, or any woman, would want to spend five minutes with him, much less years.

"She doesn't want to do that," he says then, before Liv has a chance to reply.

"Liv?"

"I can take care of myself," she says. "I don't exactly need a babysitter." She thumps herself down on the couch.

"See? What did I tell you?" says her father.

Sam stands between Liv and her father, looking first at him, then at her. She wants to do something, say something, *fix* things. She is that kind. "Well, good night, you two," she says finally. Then: "Fight nice."

Liv almost giggles. *Fight nice?*

The door closes behind her. "Life is never what it seems," says Rod Serling, "in the world of the Twilight Zone . . ." Sam's car starts on the second try. Liv listens to the tires backing over gravel, the motor idling as Sam brakes and then turns the heavy car toward the main street. Then she is gone.

She sneaks a look at her father. He is asleep, his head laid back, mouth open, as if he had dropped off in the exact moment of saying something, maybe something very important, but of course she will never know what that was. In the flickering gray light, his face looks old and weary, and a panicky thought crosses Liv's mind that he isn't her father, after all. There has been some terrible mistake, some miscommunication, and she's been handed over to a perfect (well, hardly perfect!) stranger. It could *happen*. The only photograph Liv has of him, which she'd buried long before in a pile of photos of friends and Gran, was of a thin young man wearing a white T-shirt, standing with his legs apart and his fists on his hips, laughing up at the sun.

He is thirty-six, her father, but he looks and acts like a much older man. He seems like someone who's already lived his life and is just running down the clock. Thirty-six isn't supposed to be *that* old.

She lets herself quietly out the door. It is a dark night, just a sliver of a moon overhead, a scattershot of stars. It doesn't occur to her to be afraid, to guard her flanks as she would have in the city. This isn't a real place. She heads in the direction of the beach—the only direction if you didn't want to wander through the seedy neighborhoods or head for the freeway. She sucks greedily on the first of her two precious cigarettes, drawing smoke deep into her lungs, a good hurt, a numbness.

A single car passes, turning into an alley of small, shabby wooden houses and disappearing. She could be the last person on earth. The one lone survivor of a nuclear holocaust. But if this is true, wouldn't she have something more to worry about than where her cigarette-after-next is going to come from? She laughs. Then, since no one can hear her anyway, she laughs louder, a strangled, laughing cough. Then she throws her long arms into the air and yells, "Hey!" No answer. Only the sound of the waves hissing as she nears the beach. Where the sand starts, she shucks her boots.

The sand is cooler than she expected after so warm a day, cool and rough. She plows her way out to where the waves, iridescent in the light of a waning moon, are backing off, leaving a strip of smooth wet sand behind. It occurs to Liv then that she can just keep going, go straight across that strip of wet sand and into the water, out into the whole Pacific Ocean, and never return.

The thought is deep and dangerous, scary. The worst kind of bogeyman voice in her head. It's easy, the voice says. It's easy, then it's over.

But it is not so easy to drown. She learned that in an English class. Some writer, she can't remember who, filled her pockets with rocks so she wouldn't change her mind at the last minute. Which Liv probably would. She'd be doing it only to spite her father, who wouldn't care. So what was the sense of that?

And Gran would never, ever forgive her.

She spreads her jacket on the sand and curls up on it, hugging her knees. She needs her Gran. Missing Gran is stuck inside her chest, frozen there. It will never melt because she won't let it. That and the stupid china is all she has left. Her eyes leak like a wound. She closes them, lets sleep come on like an old friend.

"Olivia!"

The voice comes from a long way off, from the far end of a tunnel. She lets it go.

"Olivia, damn it. What the hell are you doing down here?"

A shape looms over her, blocking the moon. Liv sits up, trying to get her bearings.

"Are you nuts or what? You wanna be a statistic your first night in California?" He hands her the lizard boots.

She leans over, brushing the sand from her jeans, pulls on her boots. There are tears in her eyes, she doesn't know why, and she doesn't want him to see.

By the time she looks up, he is halfway across the sand, heading home.

6

HER FATHER IS GONE. Liv knows this the second she wakes up, something about the way an empty house feels. She had dreamed about Suds, a good dream, until Suds held the capsules out on her dark palm and said, "Here, take this. Then everything will be all right." The capsules glowed like green neon, like kryptonite. Liv woke herself up, heart pounding, and lay staring at the cottage-cheese ceiling. Suds is the last person to do a thing like that. The dream feels like a betrayal of her best friend.

She blasts her stereo and the dream scatters.

She gets up, wanders into the kitchen. Coffee cup on the counter, rinsed and upended. On the table, a note. Liv picks it up, caught by the writing more than the words. Printing. Neat, block letters, all the same size. OLIVIA: THERE IS MONEY IN THE CIGAR BOX IN THE CUPBOARD OVER THE STOVE IF YOU NEED IT. HERE'S YOUR KEY.

With the pen lying next to the note, she crosses out

"Olivia" with a big black X. Then she writes in block letters LIV and underlines it. Twice.

She rummages in a cupboard for coffee, finds a jar of instant. "Yuck!" Aloud, for company. Puts the jar back. If she's going to live in this dump, she's going to have to buy a coffeepot and some real coffee. At *least*. In the cupboard over the stove, where her father said it would be, a wooden cigar box. Inside, to her surprise (*Gran, would you believe this?*), a pile of bills, tens and twenties. She scoops out half of it.

In the bathroom her father's blue shaving kit sits on the toilet tank. Liv picks it up with the tips of her fingers and carries it back to the cardboard box under the window where the thing belongs, dropping it in.

Dressed in a black T-shirt and black jeans, Walkman, makeup, and all her silver in place, she heads out the door.

Sun so bright, it hurts.

The idea today is that this could be a vacation. She could be a tourist staying at the Hope Motel (upgraded), seeing the sights. First time in California. She could pretend. It didn't have to be anything else, not yet.

At the corner of the weed lot and the gas station, a green-and-white city bus. The driver gets out, goes around to the back of the gas station. Liv gets on the bus, drops three quarters into the box, and clomps all the way to the back. She finds an empty seat, sprawling herself out so that no one can sit next to her. Up front, a pack of loonies. Gran wouldn't like that, calling them names. Cruel, she would say. One, a fat boy-man with a crew cut, picks his nose and studies it like a lab experiment. An old lady slaps her skinny thighs and rocks back and forth. The driver comes up the steps, slings himself into his seat, and off they go. Liv figures they're headed for Santa Barbara, though she hasn't looked at the sign on the front and could be going anywhere.

An adventure.

A tourist on an adventure.

She tries for a while not to think about her father, and finally gives up. It's impossible not to. Gazing out the window at the fuzzy-looking gray-green mountains, the motels and restaurants strung out along the freeway like outposts of civilization in a grade-B Western, she thinks about the night before, how strange it was. She tries to remember how she had thought her father would look, how he would act when he saw her. What he would do. What did she expect, anyway? A big bear hug? Did she really think he'd break down on the spot and beg her forgiveness for fifteen years of nothing? Where was her head?

What she and her father have is a legal arrangement, nothing more or less than that. This makes perfect sense. He could have refused to take her—just as he'd ignored her birthday and Christmas all those years. But he didn't refuse, and so here she is. She has a roof over her head, a bed, her music, a stupid pink ballerina, and a suitcase full of city clothes with expensive designer labels. A legal arrangement. A deep-down loneliness for her friends, for Gran, mostly for her Gran. Her eyes well up with tears and she blinks them back.

The bus pulls into the transit station. The loonies get off in a pack. Liv heads out of the bus station and down toward what looks to be Santa Barbara's main street.

Who was Saint Barbara, anyway? A real saint? Probably not. Everything seems fakey here, made-for-TV. All the buildings are exactly alike, same red tile roofs, same white walls, and those bright purple flowers everywhere. No trash, no broken windows. It can't be for real.

Corner of State and Carrillo, she looks left, then right. The city has been done up for something, she doesn't know what. Bright pink flags flutter from lampposts. *Take Back the Night*, they insist in bold black letters. She almost remembers what all that means, candles, women chanting. She goes right and starts walking down State. Heads turn, at first she doesn't know why. In Manhattan, you'd have to fall down bleeding before anybody gave you a second glance, and all she is doing is walking, minding her own business. So she figures it's the makeup, the spiky hair. Everybody else looks, well, boring. Straight out of a Lands' End catalogue. Wholesome.

Outside the Roma coffee shop, there are some kids, not alternative exactly, but not old. She bums a cigarette from a guy with a tattooed lizard climbing over his shoulder. He gives her four, one for now and three "for good luck." She feels his eyes on her, checking her over, as she goes inside and gets her coffee to go.

Now she knows just what she has to do. She has a purpose. Gran would like that. Liv has decided that she must buy her father a coffeepot, a coffeepot and some real coffee. Whole beans. A grinder. She can do that. She can be generous. She can be big about things, as Gran would say.

A homecoming gift, kind of. A welcome-me gift.

Yeah, why not?

At the very least, she can introduce him to one of the finer things in life, a decent cup of coffee.

An hour and half and a dozen stores later, the exact right coffeepot. Made in Italy, it says on the bottom. Drop-dead gorgeous. The lid explodes in silvery swirls like a birthday bow. A work of art, and only sixty-five dollars. Plus twenty-four something for the beans and grinder. Then there's the tax, which she somehow always forgets to count in.

Liv peels bills from the wad she found in the cigar box, no longer a wad. Back out into the street. The sun that assaulted her earlier now seems an embrace as she climbs back onto the city bus with her prize and heads for "home." Not even the brown dullness of her father's apartment can dampen her mood as she stows the pot, the grinder, and the beans in an empty kitchen cupboard. In the morning she will make her father a pot of real coffee.

She calls Suds, who's just gotten home from summer school. They talk for an hour or so. Talking to her best friend is supposed to make her feel better, but it doesn't. It only makes the whole thing more real, like writing in her journal, which she hasn't yet done. She tells Suds all about the gorgeous coffeepot, but Suds doesn't really get what Liv's trying to do. So then Liv doesn't either.

Out again to the liquor store midway down the main street.

The clerk is an old man with eyes like baggy underwear. "ID," he says.

"ID?" she cries, offended. "You've got to be kidding!"

"No ID, no cigarettes."

"But I'm twenty-three. Nobody asks for my ID anymore."

He stares at Liv with his underwear eyes, bored, already thinking of something else, the pea soup or some other yucky thing that he will heat in the microwave for his sorry lunch.

"Look," she says, man-to-man, girl to man, "I'm not trying to buy a six-pack or a porno magazine. Come on, all I want is a pack of Pall Malls."

"Tell the judge," he says, turning away.

7

SHADING HER EYES, Liv peers through the green-and-gold looping letters of Shear Magic. There, in the third station from the window, winding a pink plastic roller up a length of bleached blond hair, is Sam. Liv looms up behind her in the mirror, all silver spiky and black. The hand of the lady getting the perm goes up to rest on her heart.

"Hi, Liv!" Swipe of greenish eye shadow and glossy coral lipstick. Sam's copper-colored curls swept up into a rhinestone clip. "Out slummin'?"

"I bought my father a coffeepot," she says, embarrassed now. What had seemed like such a terrific idea doesn't sound like much all of a sudden.

"You did?" Eyes meet in the mirror. Sam grins.

"Yup."

"What a nice thing to do! Really!" Sam stretches a net cap over the pink plastic rolls. "Liv just moved here from New York," she says, to explain how this apparition in black could be standing in a place like Shear Magic. Sam's client has not been able to take her eyes off Liv's face, or maybe it's from the eleven studs in Liv's right ear.

"Think I could borrow a smoke?" Liv says.

The lady in the chair frowns, then goes after a piece of lint on the knee of her polyester slacks.

"Sure, hon," says Sam, a clip between her teeth. She nods at a set of plastic drawers. "In the bottom." Liv rummages around Sam's straw bag for the red-and-white pack, thinking she'll take three or four. She takes only two and feels very good about herself.

"I'm making us a dinner tonight," Sam says. "Well, let's say I'm *doing* dinner. On the boat. Tell your dad, okay?"

Liv finds herself waiting as night comes on, pacing the worn brown carpet. She calls Suds. This time they talk until the room is dark, taking apart Megan's new boyfriend, piece by piece, like the seagulls with a shred of dead fish. Liv switches on the light. On the arm of the sofa a saucer with lipstick-smeared cigarette butts.

She hears the truck, peeks out between the drapes. "It's him," she breathes into the phone, "gotta go!" She hangs up and grabs the saucer, dashes to the bathroom, where she dumps the butts into the toilet and flushes. Rinses the saucer.

She opens the door, which she should have done before to let the smoke out. There's her father coming across the lot. Same slogging walk, same pail in his hand.

"Got us a bug," he says. No hello, no "Hi, how're you doing, Liv? How was your day?"

So she doesn't greet him either. This is the way it will be. Because of him, because of the way he is. "A bug?"

"Lobster," he says. Steps into the room. Sniffs the air. "You smoking in here?"

"Well"—a shrug—"yeah . . ."

Straight in the eyes, like venom. "Well, *don't*."

Liv slams into her bedroom, throws herself down on the narrow bed. On her back, arms crossed over her eyes. *God!*

She will call Suds again. Beg the Molinas to let her stay with them, even though Suds doesn't have her own room, even though they already have five kids, even though Suds's brother hits on her, on Suds, his own sister. In the city, *her* city, Liv could get a job, then her own place. She doesn't *need* to be here!

In spite of herself, she listens to her father in the kitchen. There's the banging of a heavy pot. The faucet runs for a long time. Liv plays Led Zeppelin full-blast, until it fills her head too full to hold anything else.

After a while she gets up and leaves her room, fists stuffed deep into the pockets of her jeans. She wants to see Sam's boat, anything but stay here.

Standing at the sink, her father has the lobster pinched between his fingers.

"What are you doing?" she asks, before thinking that she *knows* what he's doing, of course she knows. On the hot plate boiling water bubbles in a pot.

"Did you work the Ranch today, hon?" Sam pokes her fork around her plate. She hasn't eaten much.

Liv's father has put away enough for a family of six. He reaches for the sweet-and-sour pork, dumps it on a mound of fried rice. "Yeah," he says, "couldn't find the reef, though. Damned if somebody didn't jump my spot!"

"The Ranch is up north, Liv," Sam explains. "About an hour. It's a gorgeous place, we don't know who owns it, but it's where your dad dives most of the time." She shovels what's left of the food into a single carton and fits the top together. "How's the kid, the new one—what's his name?—working out?"

In the amber overhead light her father's eyes are golden brown, which would be nice if they weren't so bloodshot. With a sizzle of shock, Liv realizes they are *her* eyes. His forehead, *her* forehead. All this makes her heart beat faster. Why?

"Spinelli, Spicoli, I don't know . . ." Her father waves his hand as if he's shooing a fly. "No, he's not working out. Doesn't want to work. Wants to learn to dive, that's all."

"You've got to find a good tender," Sam says, green eyes worried. "It's dangerous to dive without a tender, Mark. You know that."

"Well, if you find one who wants to work for a living, let me know," he says. "I've gone through three in the last six months." He stretches and yawns, rubs his face. "I'm beat."

Sam reaches across the little table, grabs his wrist, and squeezes it. Says something with her eyes into his that Liv can't read. Maybe it's about sex. About having no sex because Liv's here. Whatever. Liv does not want to pursue that line of thought, which if pursued would make her sick.

Going "home" in the truck that smells of fish guts and that rubbery smell, mixed with smoke from a leaky exhaust. "What I said about you getting a job," her father says after a long silence.

"Yeah?"

"I didn't mean to *discourage* you, what I said . . ." Watching the road all the time, not her. Steering one-handed at the bottom of the wheel.

"Don't worry about it," she says automatically.

Nothing more until they turn into the lot. Then: "That's what fathers are supposed to do, right?"

"Huh?"

"Worry," he says.

She looks at him, blinks. "Uh, yeah. I guess." Then she shrugs, an exaggerated, careless shrug. "How would I know?"

Several heartbeats later: "I guess you wouldn't," he says.

can't read. Maybe it's about sex. About having no sex because Liv's here. Whatever. Liv does not want to pursue that line of thought, which if pursued would make her sick.

Going "home" in the truck that smells of fish guts and that rubbery smell, mixed with smoke from a leaky exhaust. "What I said about you getting a job," her father says after a long silence.

"Yeah?"

"I didn't mean to *discourage* you, what I said . . ." Watching the road all the time, not her. Steering one-handed at the bottom of the wheel.

"Don't worry about it," she says automatically.

Nothing more until they turn into the lot. Then: "That's what fathers are supposed to do, right?"

"Huh?"

"Worry," he says.

She looks at him, blinks. "Uh, yeah. I guess." Then she shrugs, an exaggerated, careless shrug. "How would I know?"

Several heartbeats later: "I guess you wouldn't," he says.

"Did you work the Ranch today, hon?" Sam pokes her fork around her plate. She hasn't eaten much.

Liv's father has put away enough for a family of six. He reaches for the sweet-and-sour pork, dumps it on a mound of fried rice. "Yeah," he says, "couldn't find the reef, though. Damned if somebody didn't jump my spot!"

"The Ranch is up north, Liv," Sam explains. "About an hour. It's a gorgeous place, we don't know who owns it, but it's where your dad dives most of the time." She shovels what's left of the food into a single carton and fits the top together. "How's the kid, the new one—what's his name?— working out?"

In the amber overhead light her father's eyes are golden brown, which would be nice if they weren't so bloodshot. With a sizzle of shock, Liv realizes they are *her* eyes. His forehead, *her* forehead. All this makes her heart beat faster. Why?

"Spinelli, Spicoli, I don't know . . ." Her father waves his hand as if he's shooing a fly. "No, he's not working out. Doesn't want to work. Wants to learn to dive, that's all."

"You've got to find a good tender," Sam says, green eyes worried. "It's dangerous to dive without a tender, Mark. You know that."

"Well, if you find one who wants to work for a living, let me know," he says. "I've gone through three in the last six months." He stretches and yawns, rubs his face. "I'm beat."

Sam reaches across the little table, grabs his wrist, and squeezes it. Says something with her eyes into his that Liv

He doesn't answer. Drops the lobster, squirming, into the boiling water.

"God!" Liv cries. "Why did you *do* that?"

The grin is only in his eyes. "Do what?"

"*Kill* it. Like that!"

"It's kinder, Olivia," he says matter-of-factly. "Some things are better done quick."

"Will you please call me Liv? I hate Olivia!"

"It's a good name," he says.

She watches the poor lobster turning a darker red, which is how she's always seen them before. On a plate, in a restaurant. Drawn butter, *civilized*. "Did you rip its claws off?"

"Pacific lobster." He explains, rinsing out the pail. "They don't have claws."

"They must be pretty easy to catch, then."

He studies her face. He doesn't know her, doesn't know when she's kidding, when she isn't. His thin damp hair is plastered to his head, he needs a shave. "Try it sometime," he says. "Then you'll know."

"No, thanks." After a minute, watching the lobster boil to death, "Sam wants us to come for dinner."

"Hmmph," her father says, whatever that means.

She heads for her room. *If* she stays here, she's going to have to get a phone, her own phone.

"Well? Are we going or not?" Her father like a block of stone in the doorway to the kitchen, the light outlining the shape of him. The apartment no longer smells of smoke.

Now it smells like him, like salt water and something else, like old tires, like rubber. Rubber and cooked lobster. What does her father do out there all day? Maybe she could go with him once. Just once, for something to do.

But he probably wouldn't take her, and she sure as hell won't ask.

Sam's boat is smaller than the one Liv pictured in her mind, the white cabin cruiser she's seen in ads for cigarettes or liquor. From the outside *Lady Lore* looks smaller than Liv's bedroom. It's a cute boat, if boats can be cute. It's made of real wood that glows in the light of the sun setting at the far end of the harbor behind a row of brightly colored flags. Flag *city*!

Lady Lore has lace curtains hanging in her windows. A green canvas tarp is rigged up over the back like a tent, rolled up tonight as Liv steps from the edge of the slip and over the side into Sam's bedroom, a hodgepodge of fat pillows, a mattress on the floor covered with an Indian-print spread.

Her father follows. He's brought the lobster, wrapped carefully in foil and plastic bags.

Sam calls from the galley, "Make yourselves t'home."

Liv's father runs his hand over the wood that frames the doorway and frowns. "Didn't you say you got the teak refinished?"

"Huh?" from the galley.

"This wood is blistered. Come here. Look."

"Hang on," Sam sighs. Pops her head through the doorway, looks. "Oh, that. Yeah, well. I called the guy, but he never called back . . ." She ducks into the galley. "I got Chinese," she says, as if that's going to fix everything. "Liv, what do you drink? Coke? Iced tea?"

"You just can't let things like this go." He's too big for the boat. Can't stand straight without bending his head.

"I know, I know . . ."

He treats them both like children.

"Iced tea," Liv says, coming between them. "Please."

"So, Liv!" Sam says, dipping a chunk of the lobster into melted butter. "What did you do today?" They are stuffed into Sam's little booth-thing, she and Sam on one side, her father on the other. Open boxes of sweet-and-sour pork, fried rice, chop suey.

Sam *knows* about the coffeepot, why is she asking? "Messed around," Liv says. Her father watches her, his eyes unreadable. "I looked for a job," she adds. He can't read her the way Gran could, so what's the difference what she says?

"Oh? Where?" Sam's the type who will believe anything, but her father surely isn't.

"That place we had lunch. You know, with the surfboards."

"Any luck?"

"Nuh-uh."

Her father hasn't taken his eyes off her face. It's beginning to make her itch. "You actually think somebody's going to hire you? Looking like *that*?" He wipes the grease from his mouth, stares at her with his bloodshot eyes.

"Mark . . ." Sam warns. Now it's Sam who comes between Liv and her father. Gently. With love in her eyes, which is hard for Liv to understand.

"*What?* She wants to get a job, right?" Eyebrows go up, hands go up, like *what's the matter with all of you?* "Would you hire this kid in your beauty shop? Ha! Now wouldn't *that* be something?" He chuckles to himself, shaking his head. Snaps open a lobster tentacle, sucks out the meat.

"Maybe," Sam says, her arm nudging Liv. "We can't keep doing the same old things the same old way." Her smile teases. "Liv's the future."

He snorts. "Well then, God help us."

Liv blocks him out, pokes at her food. She is an expert with chopsticks. Her father and Sam both use forks. The chopsticks make her feel superior.

Sam starts to get up. "Coffee?"

Liv says no, thank you. Her father says, "Not for me."

"Well!" Sam says.

They both look at her, but that's all she says.

"Deep subject," Liv and her father say at the exact same time. Their eyes meet, he looks embarrassed.

Sam laughs. "Like father, like daughter, huh?"

Liv almost says, "I hope not!" Stops herself. Because she's not like him, she's not *mean*.

Between words, the sound of chewing, like sheep in a field.

8

INSIDE, SHE GOES STRAIGHT to her room and shuts the door, plops down on the chenille spread. She can still hear the TV noise. Her father can sit in that ugly brown chair for hours, hardly moving, picking abalone shells with a bug sticker—one of those needle-like things they had in biology to dissect that awful cat. He picks the white hard stuff off the backs of the shells without looking, watching the TV with creepy burned-out eyes.

If she had a phone in here, she could call Suds. Really, she should call Megan, whom she hasn't called at all.

She opens the book of Yeats poems Mr. Denker gave her on the last day of school. She was the only one in the class who liked Yeats and wasn't afraid to say so.

"I don't know if these poems will *speak* to you right now," Mr. Denker said on that last day, "what you're going through. I just wanted you to have them." And then that sweet, sad smile. "Let me know how you're doing, Liv." Mr.

Denker's wife, Dina—Dina Denker, what a name!—is going to have a baby in a few months. Mr. Denker—Phil—will be the best father. A little geeky, but that's okay. Compared to what *she's* got.

She kicks off her boots. Still dressed, she hunches on the edge of the bed, looks around the gloomy room that isn't yet hers, that never could be.

Then she's thinking about Gran again, the way she always does before bed. Gran tucked her in at night. From before Liv can remember, until the night before she died. It didn't matter that Liv was fifteen, grown. Gran would always come, always knock softly on Liv's door. "Are you asleep?" Liv would sometimes pretend she was, especially if she'd been drinking. She'd bury her head and feel Gran's kiss on the top of her head, then the fussing with the blankets to do the "tucking in." If Liv came home late, later than they'd agreed was all right, Gran would wait for Liv to settle in, never too long. Then she'd knock, come in, and sit on the edge of Liv's bed. That's all, just sit there. And Liv knew that Gran would stay just like that, all night if need be, until Liv admitted to breaking their agreement. "Even grandmothers need their beauty sleep," Gran would say. She was never angry. Worried, but never angry. It was enough to keep Liv on a straighter path than anybody but Suds.

On the breakfast table some of those mornings, articles or news stories about the dangers of smoking, of drinking, of hanging out in the clubs (how did Gran know that's where they went?). No lecture. Information. And those eyes, Gran's eyes, that knew everything.

Tears run down both sides of her face and down her neck, a cold tickle. How can she just go on as if her life hasn't cracked open like a raw egg?

Her tiny room is a prison, the windows high and narrow, like slit eyes. You couldn't get out to save your life, if you had to.

She pulls on her boots. This time she'll ask her father if she can go out. If he's so *worried* . . .

He's asleep in his chair, chin dropped to his chest, the bug sticker loose in his fingers. She tiptoes past him, opens the door carefully, steps out into the night.

She likes the beach at night, so there's *something* to look forward to. Some place to go. She walks to the end of the string of apartments, across the loose gravel, kicking through the stones.

In the end apartment somebody is yelling, cursing, a man. Deep voice. The apartment door bursts open, a woman runs out, her dark eyes glazed and frightened. The man is right behind her. They both stop, stare at Liv, frozen. The woman moves a little toward the man. Liv passes, her head down. None of her business. Just like New York.

What is she going to do for the rest of the summer? If her father is right, that nobody will hire her looking the way she does, what then? It's not like you can change your image overnight. And anyway, she likes who she is. She even likes the effect she has on people out here. In the second they do that double-take thing, she's in control. She's her own person, her own island.

Tonight she has the beach, at least this stretch of it, all to herself again. She plods out over the sand, climbs up onto the orange lifeguard tower. Sits on the edge of it with her boots dangling, hunched forward on the palms of her hands, and stares out at a necklace of lights strung across the dark horizon of the water. Oil platforms. In the daytime they look like they shouldn't be there, but at night they're pretty. Time passes, she hardly knows how much, the waves shush in and out. She's lulled into a half-sleep.

Jolted awake! The beach is lit up, flooded suddenly with white light. Liv whips around and sees black figures like cardboard cutouts, the silhouette of a car; then the light is in her eyes, too bright to see. She raises a hand to shield her eyes, to try to see what's there.

A bullhorn voice. "You! On the tower! Get down. This is the police."

Heart hammering, Liv climbs down. Stands there in the light, not knowing what to do. Put her hands up?

They come toward her over the sand, the powerful light bobbing in the hand of the one on the right.

"Let's see your ID," says the other one, the taller one, not much older than she is. Bucktoothed, skinny.

"I don't have one. I didn't do anything!"

"Name?" He slides a notebook and a golf pencil out of his shirt pocket.

Liv tells him her full legal name: Olivia Jean Trager.

He looks up from the notebook, closes it without writing anything down. "Your father is worried about you. We'll take you home."

"He *called* you? He actually sent the *cops* after me?"

She trudges through the sand behind the two policemen. She can't believe this! Gran never would have called the police. She knew Liv was safe. Had a sixth sense about it, she said. And that was in New York City! Her father must be a control freak or something.

"He's not my real father, you know."

This slows the taller one down. He turns. "Stepfather?"

"No, he just *says* he's my father. He's a . . . He's just this guy . . ." The words trail dangerously. "He uses my name, that's all. He says he's Mark Trager, right?"

The policemen exchange quick looks.

The shorter cop opens the back door of their car and she slides in. The tall one is the driver, the short one talks into the microphone. She hears her name, her father's name. There's this huge gun sticking up between the seats.

They cruise the three short blocks to Hope Avenue, Liv locked in the back like a criminal. Is this the way it's going to be now? She tries to be her own person and he sends the cops?

The car turns into the lot of Hope Apts and Motel and parks smack in the middle. The cops both get out. The short one opens the back door for Liv. Both cops follow her. "That's okay," she says. "I'm safe now." But they don't go away.

At the door to Number 5, the tall one holds her back, the short one raps the door with his nightstick.

Liv's father opens the door halfway, sticks his head out. "Yeah," he says.

"Mr. Trager? Mr. Mark Trager?"

"Yes."

"Is this your daughter, sir?"

"Yes, that's my daughter." He opens the door wider.

"May we see some ID, please."

Her father frowns. "ID?"

"She says she's not your daughter. We need to see some form of identification before we can release her to you."

His head pokes out the door, like a turtle's out of its shell. *"Liv?"*

Liv stares down at the toe of her boot.

"I'll get you your ID," her father says, fuming, his voice tight as knotted rope. "I'll do better than that!" He slams the door.

"Does he own a gun?" the tall cop asks. Glances at the shorter one.

"Put her back in the car," the short one says, but before that can happen, her father opens the door. The short cop has his gun half out of its holster. Liv watches in disbelief. In New York her father would have already been shot. The cop points his gun at her father's chest, his arm straight out. The taller cop has pulled Liv back. She wants to tell the truth then, but it's all happening too fast for that. "Put your hands up, sir," the cop orders.

"But . . ." Liv's father slowly raises his hands. "What the hell is going on? Here's her birth certificate!" He waves a piece of paper. "It's what I went to get."

The tall cop steps forward, pats her father down, finds his wallet, takes the paper out of his hand.

"That's what it is, all right," he says. "State of New York . . . mother, Jean Howard Trager . . . father, Mark Allen Trager. He's her old man, all right." The tall cop hands back the birth certificate with the wallet. The short one holsters his gun.

"Sorry, sir," he says, "but we gotta be careful. There was a rape and murder near here couple of weeks ago. Some drifter. Maybe you read about it?"

"Yeah, I heard." He frowns. Won't look at Liv now at all.

"Well, we'll leave you two to sort things out."

They turn and head for their car. The microphone crackles. Liv stalks past her father.

"You got anything to say to me?" His voice booming in that small room.

She turns at her door. "Sorry." She is sick with sorry, but she can't tell him, *won't* tell him.

Fists on his hipbones. Looking straight at her as if he still can't believe what's just happened. "Did you *say* that? Did you actually tell them I wasn't your old man?"

She stares at the floor, stain on the brown carpet in the shape of Rhode Island, or maybe it's Connecticut.

She hears him sigh, as if the wind has left him flat and drifting. "Would that make things better?" he says at last. "Is that what you want?"

She looks up. Cautiously. Like an animal peering out of its burrow. Watches him rub his forehead, run his hand over the slicked-down, thinning hair. There's no way to answer this question. Yes. Yes/no. "Do I have a choice?"

He thinks about this. His face never changes: the tired expressionless eyes, the set of his jaw, the hard planes of his wind-reddened cheeks. "You always have a choice."

"But I don't! I *didn't*! Where else could I go?" She catches her breath in a sob, clutches herself at the waist. Coming loose inside like scattered marbles.

"This is where you belong," he says quietly. He watches, stands there and watches her falling apart, his big hands dangling.

She stomps into the bathroom, makes an angry grab for a wad of toilet paper, blows her nose.

He's there in the same spot when she comes out.

"How come you have . . . *that*?" Arms crossed over her chest, Liv nods at her birth certificate lying on a stack of his folded shirts.

He turns, sees what she's talking about. "Because I'm your father," he says slowly, as if she's deaf or slow.

"You've had it all this time?" Her voice gone small.

"Yes."

"How come Gran didn't have it?"

"She had a photocopy."

"Oh."

They stare at each other some more.

He pinches his mouth with his cupped hand, sighs through his nose. "Do you want to go somewhere? Is that the problem? I know you can't just hang around here all the time." His hand waves through the brown space. "Maybe when you get some friends . . ." Stringing so many words together at a time seems to make him very uncomfortable. He rubs his chin, scratches the back of his neck.

"Go somewhere? Where? Where the hell is there to go?"

"I don't know . . ." He scowls at her, as if this is all too much, and all her fault. "We could get a beer . . . I mean, a Coke or something. If you want . . ."

Him and her? Does he really mean it? She shrugs. "Well, sure."

"But not tonight. It's late and I've gotta work . . ."

"Well, yeah!" She throws up her hands. "You *gotta* work!" In her brat voice.

"*Somebody's* gotta work!" He runs a big hand over his face. "Aw, what's the difference . . ." he mumbles, heading for the kitchen. She hears the fridge open, the grating sound of a pop-top. The fridge slams shut. She goes into her room and closes the door.

She writes seven pages in her journal, furiously scribbling in handwriting that doesn't even look like her own.

9

DAYS PASS, THEN WEEKS, like open yawning mouths. Liv sleeps until noon. She goes to the beach, walks along the lacy edge of the waves, sketches in her journal. Writes about how bored she is.

She has lunch with Sam sometimes. Sandwiches on the beach, or they eat at the Surf Hut, where Liv's made a friend of the guy who works there. His name is George and he's a little geeky, but she's glad to find somebody who speaks her own language, sort of.

Sam doesn't speak her language, but Sam is different. She doesn't judge Liv in the way most grownups do. She makes it clear when she doesn't agree with something Liv does or says, but lets her know in the way she would probably let a friend know.

"You're too much the same, you and your dad," Sam says. She and Liv are sitting on the seawall eating bologna sandwiches.

"What? No way! I'm not like him!" A clump of bread sticks in her throat.

"Oh no?" Sam looks amused, but Liv is fuming. "Just in the good ways," she quickly adds.

"Ha! Like what! The guy doesn't have a heart!"

"You just don't know him yet, Liv. I told you it would take a while." She pauses, sighs. "I know how it is . . ."

Liv studies Sam as Sam looks out toward the sea, her soft chin and pug nose, the sandy spikes of her eyelashes behind the ugly rhinestone sunglasses. "Were you and your dad alike? Is that how you know?"

Sam turns. "Nope. Not even close. It was my ma. Me and her fought like, well, like cats and dogs. Only we were both cats!" She chuckles, remembering.

The beach is full of people. Almost as many people as gulls. The sky is a stretched white canvas, the sun a blowtorch. Sam lays down her sandwich, digs into her bag for a tube of zinc oxide. Paints her nose white with it. "Just a little on your nose," she pleads, but Liv squirms away. "Just like your old man," Sam mutters. "You think because you have that olive skin you won't fry, or get skin cancer, but that's just not true."

Which keeps them talking about fathers and daughters, mothers and daughters.

"I probably shouldn't tell you this, but I gave up on my family when I was sixteen." Sam gazes out at the sunsplashed waves for several seconds, then at Liv. "Left home. I don't know why. It really wasn't so terrible there. Just this constant . . . *bickering*. But I was a pretty wild kid and thought I knew everything . . ."

Liv's intrigued. "How . . . wild?"

Sam laughs. "Consider the times. My high school class graduated the day after Bobby Kennedy was shot. 1968. I wasn't there, of course. I was in Berkeley by then, living in People's Park."

"Living in a park? Like *outside*?"

"Oh, sure. There were lots of us, all camped out like . . . like *indigenous peoples*. That's what we said. Indigenous peoples!" A slow shake of her head as she remembers. "Can you imagine?"

"So you never graduated?"

"Nope." Sam examines her coral fingernails, works of art to Liv, who paints her ragged nails black, mostly to hide them. "Went to City College for a while—they'll take anybody, all you have to be is eighteen. Then I figured I'd better find something to do to support myself. And so"—she smiles—"Beauty School."

A blue beach ball lands at Liv's feet. She tosses it back to its owner, a curly-headed angel child. "You like it? Cutting hair and stuff?"

Sam's grinning at the child, who toddles off with the ball, then drops flat on its diapered bottom. "Well, yeah. Yes. I like the creative part of it. It gets old, like anything else. But it's a living."

"I've been thinking about school," Liv says.

"Already? You've got a lot of summer left." Sam nibbles at her sandwich. That first day with the cheeseburger, Liv figured her for a big eater, but she isn't one.

70

"What if I didn't go?" Liv says slowly, forming the words with her thoughts. "I mean, you know, did what you did?"

"Oh, Liv, no!" Sam's hand on Liv's shoulder squeezes hard. "I didn't mean . . . I mean, it was *not* a good idea, definitely not a good idea, what I did! I cut my choices down to, well, down to almost nothing. I was a pretty smart kid once upon a time, believe it or not. Best speller in the county in the sixth grade."

"Yeah?"

"Don't act so surprised! Inside the heads of most hair stylists you will find a living, working brain. Honest."

Liv laughs. "I know you're smart."

"But only because I said so! I got nothing to prove it. Liv, dropping out of school is about the dumbest thing a person can do. And if you're college material—which you most definitely are—then you've got to do the whole nine yards. Even grad school, maybe. Then you get to do what you want. *Anything* you want. Do you know how great that is? Being able to make that kind of choice in your life?"

Liv picks at the polish that's left on her thumbnail. She doesn't know. All she knows is what it feels like not to have a choice.

"Well, see, there I go lecturing." Sam brushes crumbs from her slacks, wraps up the rest of her sandwich. "For later," she says.

"It's okay," Liv says quickly. "What you call a lecture. Gran did the same thing. I guess you can miss getting lectured at."

Sam chuckles. "Well, there's plenty more where that came from."

On the way back to Shear Magic, Sam lights her last cigarette, taking a long drag and passing it over to Liv. "How's things with you and your dad?"

"The same."

"Which means?"

"You know," Liv says, "he works, he sleeps, he picks at his shells, he works, he sleeps . . ."

"Yeah, I know." Then: "Did you ever make him that coffee?"

Liv throws up her hands in a helpless gesture. "He gets up in the *dark!*"

"Hmmm . . ." Sam ponders this as if it's a serious problem. "I guess you can't make it the night before, huh?"

Liv explains what Sam obviously doesn't know. "You have to grind the beans, fresh. That's the whole point!"

Sam suppresses a smile just starting at the corners of her mouth. "I see."

"Well," Liv says, still thinking about the coffee, "I suppose I *could* make it the day before. He could warm it up in the morning. Anything would be better than that instant stuff."

"Absolutely," Sam says, just like Gran, as if she's perfectly serious.

That afternoon Liv takes out the coffeepot. She holds it in her cupped hands, admiring it all over again in the dim yellowish kitchen light. She grinds some beans, assembles the pot, and puts it on the hot plate. Soon the smell of fresh coffee floods the apartment. After she's poured some into an empty peanut butter jar and stowed it in the fridge, Liv walks back to Shear Magic to tell Sam. For something to do.

But Sam's not there.

"Boob check," Helen explains. "Mammogram. She hates 'em. Kept putting it off until I told her she'd be out of a job if she didn't go. Of course, I didn't mean it. She knew that. But it worked. My mother died of breast cancer, so did Sam's. When you're over forty, you can't afford to mess around."

Liv stops at the Surf Hut on the way back home, leans her arms on the counter of the take-out window. George is inside, wiping a dirty wet rag over the ice cream machine. "Hey, George," she says. "You think I could get a job here? You know, couple of days a week?"

He glances at her, bites his lower lip. His earlobes turn a bright pink. "Geez, I don't know, Liv. Like if it was up to me, sure! But the boss, he's, well, he'd take one look at you and . . . *freak*!" He wrings out the rag, drapes it over the edge of the sink. "I mean, not that there's anything wrong with the way you look . . ." Now his whole face is pink.

"Yeah," Liv says. "Right. Well, I don't need the money, anyway. My Gran left me a bundle. I just thought, you know, for something to do."

"Yeah," he says. He's so ready to believe anything she tells him. Truth is, whatever money there is from the sale of the flat will go straight into a college fund. If Liv doesn't use it, then the money goes to Emma Woods, the private school Liv attended until the tenth grade. Some of the money will go to Emma Woods in any case. Only fair, since Liv went there on scholarship.

She hangs out at the Surf Hut, sketching and writing. At first everything she wrote in her journal was about her life in New York, how much she missed it. About Gran and how she missed her, missed everybody from "home." Now it's mostly about Sam and her father, and about how much her life has changed. Figuring all that out, or trying to. There are sketches of the beach, of gulls in flight or lined single-file along the edge of the water, their beaks to the wind. She even drew a sketch of the dumpy apartment building that she photocopied and sent to Suds.

Suds doesn't write much, neither does Megan. Hard as it is sometimes to believe, life goes on.

10

ONE NIGHT HER FATHER COMES HOME without his pail. "I'm taking you to the John Dory," he announces. "You got something to wear . . . besides *that*?" He means the whole thing, the black jeans and T-shirt, the makeup, the hair. It's clear by the way he looks her over.

Liv's chin goes up, just like her Gran. "You got something to wear besides *that*?"

Her father looks down at his rumpled plaid shirt, his damp wrinkled jeans, torn at the knees. Looks up at her again, as if he really doesn't get it. *"What?"*

"I'll change my shirt," she sighs. Goes into her room, digs out a white T-shirt. Nothing printed on the back, one of the few.

He almost smiles when she comes out of her room.

The balcony of the John Dory hangs out over the sidewalk, big orange neon OPEN sign in the window, yellow-and-black awnings. Beneath the balcony, fishing boats with wide decks, tangles of net, green glass floats. The air smells of fresh fish and gasoline. Liv trudges up the narrow stairway behind her father.

Inside, the dining room is jammed full and smoky. Liv watches the hostess's mouth move but can't hear what she says over the noise of the crowd and Frank Sinatra. The hostess knows her father, Liv can see that. She actually *flirts* with him, and she's *young*! Then she spots Liv standing behind him and her face freezes. They're led to a small round table on the balcony.

Her father sits. He's too big for the chair. He hangs his arm on the brass rail, looks out over the harbor as if he owns it. "One of the few working harbors left," he says. "All the rest are full of crap. Kiddie rides. Taffy booths, shell shops. Crap!" He waves a hand, dismissing it. "Get the chowder," he says, as she opens the menu. "It's good."

So of course she doesn't order the chowder.

Waiting for their food to come, they both gaze out over the harbor so they won't have to look at each other. He explains things to her like a teacher. "That's sea urchins," he says, pointing at a huge net full of dark spiny things being hoisted from the *Hannalori*. "They'll ship the roe to Japan. There's a big market for it there."

Liv lays her arm along the brass rail, rests her chin on it. "I guess they're easy to catch, huh?"

"They're the pits," he says darkly. "Those spines get into your fingers, you've got a major infection."

"Oh."

"Yeah, they're easy enough to get. Like weeding. You just walk around on the bottom, picking them." He shakes his head in disgust. "I guess I'll be doing it before long . . ."

"Yeah? How come?"

"The abalone's almost gone. Fished out. Between the divers and the otters, there's not much left. That's why I go all the way up the—"

"Hey, Tug! Big guy!" A huge man with a frizzy red beard comes up behind Liv's father and claps him hard on the shoulder.

Tug?

"Who's your date?" The bearded man grins big, missing teeth.

Her father looks annoyed, but the look passes. "This is my kid, my *daughter*, Olivia. Olivia, this is Charlie." He frowns across the table at Liv. "Don't believe anything this man tells you, Liv. No matter what he says." But he's not serious, it's easy even for her to see that.

Charlie's booming laugh makes every head turn. "You old son-of-a . . ." He glances at Liv and stops himself. "*B*. Son-of-a-b! I'm the *good* guy! I came out here to invite you two to come inside and eat with us. I'm buyin'."

"See what I mean, Liv? Watch what happens when the check comes."

"Honest to God," Charlie swears, making an X across his faded green Grateful Dead T-shirt. His graying red hair is stringy and hangs almost to his shoulders. "I hit paydirt on Tuesday. Found me a reef that wouldn't quit!"

Liv's father gets very still. "Oh? Where?"

Charlie hesitates for a fraction of a second. His eyes shift away, then back to Liv's father. "Now, you know I'm not going to tell you, Tug. I'm still pickin' it, what few's left."

Liv's father looks Charlie over and Liv sees something in him shift and ease. "Well, good for you." He claps a hand on Charlie's arm and shakes it hard. "Thought I had a good spot myself last week. Up at the Ranch. But somebody cleaned me out before I could get back to it."

"Jumped ya?" Charlie's eyes widen in disbelief.

"Yeah."

"Sons-of-b's," he says. "Sons-of-b's. Well, hey! Why don't you come on inside. I owe you a lot, man, and you know it. Give me a chance for a little payback time."

"Well . . ." Liv can tell he wants to. He glances over to see if it's okay with her. She shrugs. What would they have talked about, anyway? They get up and follow Charlie inside.

To Liv's surprise, her father is greeted like a returning war hero. "Tug, my man!" "Well, if it ain't ole Tug!" "Where you been keeping your bad self?" Their eyes shift around her, as if she's not exactly there.

Chairs are added to the already crowded table. Her father introduces her. Goes from his right, straight around the table to the boy on Liv's left. "And this is my worthless tender," he says. "So worthless I can't even remember his name."

The fishermen howl with delight, everybody talking at once. "How many tenders you had in the last year, Tug?

Two, three dozen?" Charlie leans around the left side of the tender, whose name her father has forgotten, to catch Liv's attention. "Nobody can work for your old man," he tells her. "If they don't bust their butts off for him, he drowns 'em. Ain't that right, Tug?" His big red face is gleeful.

"Better than shootin' 'em," her father says, starting to sound like all the others. The tension has left his face, and soon he's returning barbs as fast as they're shot his way.

"Name's Spinuchi."

Liv turns to the tender, who has stuck out his hand for her to shake.

"Well, *Brian*," he says reluctantly, "but everybody calls me by my last name."

They shake hands solemnly, each looking the other over.

"I'm sorry about"—Liv nods her head toward her father—"about him!"

"Oh, *him*!" Brian laughs. "They all warned me about your father, but I needed the work . . ."

"He's *that* bad?"

"Pretty bad." He laughs again, ruefully this time. "But you can only believe about half of what these guys say. Anyway, your dad is the best diver around. Everybody knows that. I figured I could learn from him."

Golden ringlets cover Spinuchi's head. He looks like the child she saw that afternoon on the beach, that same wide-eyed look, as if he's ready at the drop of a hat to be surprised, nicely surprised. Liv guesses he's a little older than she, sixteen maybe seventeen. Suds would be in love by now, but he's not Liv's type. And of course she couldn't be his, even though he didn't give her the kind of look she's been getting since she arrived, like she's from some alien planet.

"You gotta admire the guy," Spinuchi continues. "He's got the fastest boat, and *clean*! Man, when I get a boat, that's just how it's gonna be. The *Jeannie T.* But I guess you've been out on her, right?"

Surprise makes her stutter. "Wh-what? Huh? Oh no. I just got here. *What's* the name of his boat?"

"The *Jeannie T.*"

Liv looks down at her plate, which has gotten filled somehow with stuff from the platters: lobster, crab, shrimp. Enough food for a week, when all she ordered was a fish-burger. "That's my mom's name. Well, I mean, she's not around anymore." And then of course she has to explain the rest. "She died when I was born."

"Oh." His already wide eyes widen, and Liv's afraid for a crazy minute that he's going to cry.

"No, it's . . . it's all right. It was . . . a long time ago."

Well, duh. *Of course it was a long time ago, if I was just born!*

But Spinuchi doesn't catch it, he just looks very sad.

Charlie gets Spinuchi's attention, and Liv, nibbling on a French fry, glances over at her father. He looks happy as a kid at a birthday party. He even gives her a quick, shy smile when their eyes meet. She's too surprised to smile back.

"Where's my father's boat?" she asks Spinuchi after a while, her mind repeating—the *Jeannie T*, the *Jeannie T*. He named the boat after her mom and never changed it.

"Marina 1," he says. "You've never seen it?"

"Nope."

Spinuchi looks surprised. "Jeez, I thought . . . I mean, since you've been here a while—"

"Almost six weeks," Liv says dully. Can it really be that long?

"Well, I can show you the boat."

She glances over at her father, who's holding up his beer in a toast to something or other.

"Come on," Spinuchi says, pushing back his chair. "It's all right."

Her father turns to look as she gets up. "Where are you going?" His words are slower than usual, which is pretty slow. She figures it's the beer.

"Hawaii," Spinuchi says, with a straight face.

"Oh well, as long as you're not going far," her father says, a glimmer of humor in his dark eyes. Then: "Liv? Half an hour. I've gotta get up early."

Spinuchi puts out a hand. "Can I have the keys?"

Liv's father scowls. "What for?"

"Thought I'd show Liv the boat," Spinuchi says.

Her father leans back in his chair, frowning up at Spinuchi. "Oh, you did, did you?"

They wait while he thinks whatever he's thinking, no way to know. Liv toys with the idea that he might have wanted to show her the boat himself. But he isn't like that. He wouldn't care if she ever saw the boat.

Her father drops the keys on the table. Pushes them toward Spinuchi and dives back into the conversation with his buddies.

It's nearly dark outside, but streetlights along the breakwater cast wavery lights into the puddles along the washed sidewalk. Liv matches Spinuchi's stride, her hands stuffed into her back pockets because, for some reason, she's forgotten what else to do with them. She reads the names of the fishing boats aloud: *La Donna Maria, Mary Jane, Linda Lee*. Most are named for women, and most have middle names, not just a letter.

"That one there? *Two Brothers*. It's the oldest," Spinuchi says. "Those guys have been fishing longer than anybody around."

"Are they really brothers?"

"Yup." He grins at her, gives her a long look. She looks down and frowns, avoiding the deeper puddles. Her boots aren't exactly waterproof.

They head down a steep ramp. At a locked metal gate Spinuchi inserts a plastic card, holds the gate to let her go through first.

There are smaller boats here, some with their lights on and people aboard. "Do you know Sam? Samantha?" Liv asks. "She's my father's girlfriend."

"Seen her a couple of times. She lives down here, right?"

"Yeah, but I think it's a different place, one of the other—"

"—marinas," he finishes for her. "It's cool to live down here, I guess. If you don't mind hoofing it to the outhouse."

He explains that this marina is mainly for small diving and fishing boats, not for living aboard. "There's your dad's," he points as they near an unimpressive-looking gray boat about the size of Sam's.

"That's it?" she says, surprised that it's so small.

"Best diving boats anywhere," Spinuchi says, patting the side of the cabin. "It's a Radon, designed right here in Santa Barbara." He walks slowly around the boat, looking it over, admiring it as if he, too, is seeing it for the first time.

And there it is, across the back, *Jeannie T*, in looping black letters almost as large as the ones on the big fishing boats. She can't pull her eyes away. "I thought . . ." she says aloud, not really meaning to.

He waits, as if she's going to say something fascinating. It's kind of unnerving how patient he is.

"I just figured . . ." She frowns, thinking. "I don't know. It's been such a long time. I thought he'd probably forgotten all about her."

Spinuchi is quiet for a minute, then says, "I guess he's a little like an abalone." He laughs softly. "He mated for life."

Liv gives him an incredulous look. "You're kidding, right? About abalones?"

"Well, yeah. It's what your dad told me, but he was putting me on. Hey, did he tell you he's trying to grow abalones in tanks? It's called mariculture and—"

"He doesn't tell me anything."

He looks at her for a second or two without saying anything more. "He's a strange dude," he says.

On deck, Spinuchi points out all the boat's features. Liv's not surprised how neat everything is, all stowed in plastic crates, not a scratch on the paint as far as she can see. Even the deck looks freshly washed.

Spinuchi unlocks the cabin door and Liv follows him inside. He switches on a dim overhead light. They have to bend their heads to stand, and there's hardly room to move, but it's cozy-looking, with a neatly made-up narrow bunk. She leans over the bunk to peer at a photograph on the wall, thinking it might be her mother. But it's of her father, standing on deck, a huge fish thrashing at his bare feet.

"Blue shark," Spinuchi says. "Probably threw it back. They're not good eating."

"I guess there's lots of sharks out there, huh?"

"Tons," Spinuchi says, "but most of them won't bother you. It's the whites you have to worry about."

"Whites?"

"Yeah, you know, like in *Jaws*." In the dim light he looks older, more serious. "When you first start diving, they're all you think about. Well, all I think about . . ." He grins, embarrassed. "But they're pretty few and far between, thank God!"

"Did my father ever see one?"

Spinuchi's eyes widen just enough to let her know the answer. "Um, yeah, I think he did once—"

He turns toward the door at the same time Liv turns toward the bunk. They collide softly.

"Oops, sorry!"

"Oh! Sorry!"

They laugh, easier with each other after that. She follows him up the two steps and out onto the deck.

They walk over the creaking wooden ramps, Spinuchi's hands stuck in his back pockets, just as hers were on the way over. His arms are strong-looking, muscular, and though he is tall and thin, his shoulders are broad and angular. You probably have to be pretty strong to be a tender, to work on a dive boat.

Water laps beneath the ramp. There's a slight onshore breeze that cools the evening, and Liv, in spite of herself, is beginning to see how people could love this place. The weather, anyway. She still can't see what there is to do!

As if Spinuchi is reading her mind, he asks how she likes Santa Barbara "so far."

"It's okay," she says, "but we don't live up here."

"Yeah, I know. You live in Carp. Kind of quiet, huh? I mean, after New York and all . . ."

She looks over at him, surprised. "How did you know I lived in New York?"

"Your father told me."

"He did?" Somehow she can't imagine her father talking about her with anyone. Of course, he must have. He and Sam must have talked about her coming.

"Sure, he did. Couple of days before you came. He said

he hadn't seen you since you were born. *That* was hard to believe!"

"True, though."

"Wow," Spinuchi says, his forehead crinkled. "It must be tough—getting to know each other—after all that time."

She tries to laugh it off, but the laugh comes out like a rusty cough.

"I mean, it would be tough getting to know *my* old man after eighteen years, but *your* dad . . ." He shakes his head. "I learn stuff about him every day, though. Everybody's got a story about him. He's almost a legend around here. You already heard about him holding a tender's head underwater—"

"Did he really try to drown him?"

"Nah. Taught him a lesson is all. The guy let the compressor die. Probably dozed off. And your father's underwater and his air just cuts off! I'd get pretty ticked off, too."

"I guess . . ." She tries to picture her father underwater, the look on his face when he knows he's out of air.

"But there's all this other stuff, too. Good stuff. About him helping people out. Like Charlie. When he got pneumonia real bad and couldn't work for about six months, your dad told Charlie's wife to go ahead and use his account at Santa Cruz market. Charlie's got five kids."

"He works a lot," she says, trying to make this new information about her father fit with all the rest. "He leaves before the sun comes up every morning. Even Sunday."

"Well, he doesn't dive every day. There's a lot of chop in

the channel and you can't just dive whenever you want to. Usually he's working on somebody's engine. Half the time for free."

The gate clangs shut as they leave the marina behind.

"Charlie and some of the other guys called him Tug," Liv says. "Weird!"

"Yeah."

"Why do they call him that?"

Before Spinuchi can answer, they meet her father coming down the stairs. He is his old self, his silent self again. "We're going out tomorrow," he tells Spinuchi. "Be here on time."

Spinuchi's hands and eyebrows go up. "Have I ever been late?"

"Didn't say that. I just said be on time."

Spinuchi grins at Liv, rolls his eyes. She grins back.

"See ya," he says.

"See ya," she says.

"Don't start getting any ideas about him," her father says, climbing behind the wheel of the pickup.

Liv gets in, slams the door shut.

"He's lazy as all the rest. Soft. Afraid to get his hands dirty."

"I don't have any *ideas* about him," she says, arms crossed, slumped in the seat. "He just showed me your boat, that's all."

"Oh?"

"Yeah." She rests her boots on the dash. When he doesn't say anything, she leaves them there. "He thinks you're pretty great, you know."

"Sure he does." Bitten-off laugh.

"He *does*. Don't ask me why . . ."

He looks at her, his eyes flash, then darken with something that in somebody else's eyes might be sadness.

After he's fallen asleep in his chair, Liv tiptoes into the kitchen with a note she's written: WARM UP THE COFFEE IN THE JAR IN THE FRIDGE. LIV.

11

SOMETHING IS PULLING at her arm. She opens her eyes. In the dark, it takes several seconds to remember where she is.

"Where's the money?" A dark shape, fuzzy, indistinct, becomes the sharp outline of her father looming over her bed.

"What money?"

And then she remembers.

". . . couple of hundred bucks in that box," he says. "Where is it?"

"I don't know . . ." she mumbles, trying to escape back into sleep.

"Liv, damn it! That was supposed to last you. Where is it?"

She sits up, rubs her face. "I bought a coffeepot," she says, "and some other . . . stuff. Didn't you see my note?"

"A coffeepot?" He clicks on the overhead light. She wants to skitter for cover like a cockroach.

"Yeah, a coffeepot," she mumbles.

"We're talking hundreds of dollars," he fumes, fists locked on his hips. "What do you mean you bought a coffeepot?"

"It wasn't *that* much," she says, guessing at how many times she dipped into the box, six? seven? Well, she had to have *money*.

She gets up, pushes past her father without looking him in the eye, and goes into the bathroom. She pees, flushes. Thinks about locking herself in until he goes away.

He's waiting by the door when she comes out. "You spent it all? All the money in the box?"

"Well, yeah. What did you think? *I* don't have any money. Did you have some coffee? The coffee in the jar that I made you?"

He doesn't answer.

"Well, did you?"

"Yeah. I drank it." He scratches the back of his head.

"Well?"

"Well, *what*?"

"What did you think?"

He looks blank. "It was okay."

"Is that all? Just okay? It's fresh-ground beans!" Her fists on her hips now.

He stares at her in disbelief. "Jesus *Christ*!" he cries. He stalks out of her room, slams out of the apartment. She hears his truck start up with a low growl. Loose stones scatter beneath his tires as he guns the engine and skids onto the street.

Under the words of her note, three more: IT'S GOOD. THANKS.

She folds the note in half, then in half again. The note came before he opened the cigar box. Obviously. He wouldn't have written it if he'd known then what she'd spent the money on.

Well, what did he think? That she could live without money? It's not as if she was spending it all on herself! And it was *good* coffee. He said so!

She was going to have to get a job. The box was empty now. It probably wasn't going to fill up again either.

Maybe sixty-five dollars *was* too much for a coffeepot.

But after she makes herself some coffee, she changes her mind again. Sixty-five was a *bargain* for this pot!

Today she will definitely find a job. Somewhere.

Sam said, well almost said, she could work at Shear Magic. Maybe sweeping up hair or something.

She showers and dresses, heads for Shear Magic.

Sam isn't at her station. Helen catches a glimpse of Liv in the mirror, and her eyes shift quickly away to the blow-dry she's doing.

"Isn't Sam working today?"

"Nope," Helen says, still not looking at Liv. "She took the day off."

"Is she sick?"

Helen frowns. "No, she's all right. Just took the day off."

Liv leaves the shop. Something isn't right. Liv doesn't

know Sam all that well. Even so, she knows that Sam isn't the type to take the day off for no reason. She heads for the bus stop.

It's breezy at the harbor. The flags along the breakwater snap in the wind. Metal lines clang against masts like hundreds of rattling wind chimes. On the balcony of the John Dory a boy is sweeping, slowly, as if he's caught in a dream. Fishing boats rock in the churned-up water, creaking like old houses. At the base of the ramp Liv waits, then follows a woman with a key card and a bag filled with groceries through the gate. She makes several wrong turns, then finally finds Sam's boat.

The green awnings are down. Liv knocks on the roof. "Sam?"

A boat motors past and the *Lady Lore* rocks up and down. "Sam?"

Sam's pale freckled face in the curtained window for a second, then gone. The awning parts and Sam's face appears there. She looks sleepy, bloated.

"Are you okay?" Liv feels stupid now, as if she shouldn't have come.

"Oh, Liv," Sam sighs. "I'm sorry, hon. Come on in." She rolls up the awning, flinches at the sunlight. It's almost noon and Sam is still in her nightgown, one of those old-fashioned flannel things with lace around the neck. Her coppery hair is sprung in every direction. "I'm not feeling too hot."

Liv climbs in. The floor is a tangle of sheets and pillows. Sam starts tossing things into place.

"Helen said you weren't sick, but I was worried. You *are* sick."

"No, not really." Sam, too, is avoiding Liv's eyes. What's going on? "Oh, honey, I didn't want to worry you. That's the last thing I'd want to do . . ."

"What's wrong? Tell me." Liv's heart thumps heavily. She shouldn't have come.

Sam reaches for her cigarettes, changes her mind. She sits down on one of the overstuffed pillows, lays her head against the side of the boat for a minute, eyes closed, faint purple shadows beneath them. "I didn't want to worry you . . ."

"What?" Liv, weak-kneed, drops to one of the pillows.

Another boat passes and they rock gently while Sam considers. "There's this lump," she says, frowning. "More than one, actually." Her hand goes halfway to her chest, then settles in her lap.

"Lump?" But she knows.

"In my breast. Both breasts."

"Oh no, Sam!" Liv's eyes well up.

"I just found out yesterday. Don't say anything to your dad, okay? Not yet."

"Why? Don't you want him to know?" Liv blots her leaky nose with the side of her hand. Sam tosses her a box of tissues. Liv pulls a couple and blows, balling up the tissue in her fist.

"He worries," she says.

"My father?" Are they talking about the same person?

"Like you wouldn't believe. He'll drive me crazy, wanting to do something, to fix it!" She laughs softly.

"What are they . . . what are you going to do?" In her mind, a sudden flash to Mercy Hospital, the door to the CCU. She swallows hard.

Sam smiles sadly. "You poor kid. You don't need this right now, do you?"

Liv blinks back her tears, trying not to break down. Sam is right, this isn't something she needs. Not now, not ever. She doesn't want to see the inside of a hospital room for the rest of her life.

"They'll do some surgery. A biopsy first, then whatever. I told them, *If* it's cancer, I just want it out of there. That's all I care about." She sounds matter-of-fact, but Liv can't look at her. "Hey!"

Liv looks up. A smile on Sam's pale freckled face, worry in her green eyes.

"Come on over here." Sam pats the cushion beside her. Liv crawls over. Sam slings an arm around Liv's shoulders. "I don't want you fretting over me," Sam says. "I mean it. I'm a tough old bird, believe me." Wanting to run, needing desperately to run, Liv finds herself curling up instead, lying down, resting her head in Sam's warm flannel lap. "Women get cured of this stuff all the time. They've got some new drug, made out of this rare tree . . ."

"When?" Liv says in a small voice.

"When? Oh, the surgery? Week from Thursday."

"Are you going to tell . . . tell *him* before then?"

"Wednesday night," Sam says. "I'll tell your dad then."

"He's pissed at me," Liv says after a while.

"I know, sugar . . ."

"You know?"

"He told me this morning. When he came over this morning."

So then Liv knows why her father gets up so early. She was beginning to think he and Sam didn't have sex at all, which had begun to worry her more than the fact that they actually *did*.

"He probably won't even take the day off, that Thursday," Liv says bitterly.

"Oh, he will," Sam assures her. Her hand smooths Liv's cheek, and it's hard for Liv not to think about Gran, not to miss that other soft hand. "You know," Sam says, looking down, "I'll bet you'd be just gorgeous with reddish-brown hair."

"That's what color it is," Liv grumbles. "My real hair."

"Yeah," says Sam, "that's what I figured."

12

HER FATHER COMES HOME carrying his pail. He mutters a greeting, she mutters one back. Is it always going to be like this?

He clicks the wall switch in the kitchen. Dull yellow light floods the small room, its brown countertops and cupboards. He sets the pail in the sink. "Come here," he says. "Watch what I do with this ab, then next time you can do it."

She goes over to the sink reluctantly. Does he really think she's going to start cooking his dinner? Except for sandwiches, all she knows is how to heat a can of soup.

"Spinuchi broke his damned arm!" her father says out of nowhere.

"Oh no! How?"

"Well, I didn't do it," he says, popping the abalone from its pearly home, "if that's what you're thinking."

"What happened?" Poor Spinuchi!

"Cracked his car up. Not his fault, he says. But I doubt it. I knew he wasn't going to last . . ."

Exasperated, Liv throws up her hands. "I can't believe you!"

"What?" Sometimes he has the strangest look in his eyes, almost as if he's afraid of her.

"It's not like he did it on purpose!"

"Huh!"

"Well, don't stand there. Get the skillet."

"So what're you going to do now? Without a tender?" She puts the skillet on the hot plate, chunks off some butter, and dumps it in. She tries not to sound like Sam, like she really cares, but Sam did say that it was dangerous to dive alone.

Her father doesn't answer. His knife slides smoothly through the white flesh of the abalone. Liv cups the abalone's shell in her hands, the colors inside this one almost transparent, silvery pink and coral. Strange, she thinks, how it hides all its beauty inside.

"Sam says you're not supposed to dive without a tender. You're not going to do that, are you?"

"You be my tender," he says suddenly, laying down his knife, leaning on his palms flat on the counter, looking at her through narrowed eyes.

"Me?"

"Why not? You're a big girl. And besides, you owe me."

Without realizing, she'd been tensed up inside, waiting.

She knew he'd say something about the money, sooner or later.

"I'm going to get a job," she says. "Don't worry. I'll pay you back."

"You've got a job," he says, with an almost-grin, a challenge in his dark eyes. The abalone in the pan begins to sizzle and he flips it.

"But I don't know how to . . . do whatever it is they do!"

"Tend," he says. "They tend. I'll teach you, don't worry. You can't be any worse than the other morons."

He sets two plates on the table and slides the abalone pieces onto them. They sit.

She looks down at the bare table, at the two almost empty plates. "Shouldn't we, like, have a vegetable or something? A salad?" Two vegetables at Gran's, one green, one yellow. Gran's scalloped potatoes or her Louisiana "dirty rice." And grace, holding hands across the table.

"Good idea," he pronounces. "As soon as you've got a little money, you can buy us some food. Make us a salad. Great idea, Liv." He pops a chunk of abalone in his mouth, stabs his fork at her. "You're going to have one hell of an appetite from now on. I can tell you that!" He's laughing at her. You wouldn't be able to see it from his face, but he's laughing at her.

She slides out the chair opposite him and drops into it. "You gonna drown me, too, if I can't do it? If I can't *tend*?"

He looks down at his plate and mumbles, "If I didn't drown you at birth, I'm not about to do it now."

She picks up her fork, then sets it down carefully on her plate. "Why didn't you?"

"What? Drown you?" He looks up, his eyes guarded.

"Yeah. Instead of, you know, giving me away? Why didn't you just drown me?" Heat beats in her cheeks, her ears. She can't believe what she's just said, but it's out there burning in the air and she can't take it back.

They stare at each other silently, until finally he sets his fork down and leans back in his chair. Sighs. "That was a long time ago, Liv. God knows what I was thinking back then."

"Well, *I* know. It's pretty obvious, isn't it? You didn't want somebody you had to take care of. You didn't want a kid."

"You're probably right," he says heavily. "I was young. I don't know . . ." He gets up out of his chair, picks up his plate and fork, slice of abalone on the plate half eaten.

"You didn't want your own child." She punctuates each word like a bullet.

"I didn't say that."

"You didn't want a kid . . . you didn't want *me*! What's the difference?"

"All the difference in the world," he says. At the sink, his back to her, rinsing his plate, drying it carefully. "When Jean . . . when your mother . . ."

"Died," she says, feeling tough, angry-tough.

He turns from the sink to face her. "When your mother died," he says slowly, his face unreadable, "I became somebody el—" He stops himself, looks down at the floor. He tries again: "I tried to . . . I thought about what . . ." A muscle along his jaw spasms. "I just . . . left," he says at last.

"Yeah, well, we already know that." Her throat aching like she's swallowed hot lead.

"Finish your dinner," he tells her, not unkindly. "You're going to want to turn in early, get a full night's sleep." He walks to the door, opens it. "Anything from the liquor store?"

"Pack of Pall Malls," she spits.

"Fat chance," he says, slamming the door.

Liv stares at the yellowed wall, at a calendar from Long's Drugstore, picture of the Mission, a month out of date. He's just like the Tin Man, her father. He really has no heart.

She grabs up the phone and dials Suds, wakes her up. "Guess what!" she says. "You'll never believe what I have to do tomorrow!" She wants to sob into the phone, *Suds! Suds! Make me come home!* But she has to be stronger than that. As strong as him. The way they stare at each other! It's like some kind of contest to see who gives in first. Well, she won't! She won't let him get to her.

Liv and Suds talk until Suds, on the verge of sleep, starts to mumble nonsense.

In her bed, staring at the ceiling, trying to imagine tomorrow. She can do the work, she knows she can. *Whatever* it is! After what he's said about the others, the other *morons*, she'd die trying, that was for sure. But a whole day with him? The most they've had is an hour here and there.

At least it's something different. How bad can it be?

Then she thinks about Sam, and her heart flips over. Sick inside, she cranks on her stereo, but even her favorite songs can't drown her fears. After a while, she turns the light on and begins to write.

A knock on her door. Her father's deep voice. "Better get some sleep, Liv. The next time I knock on this door, it'll be 4:30 a.m."

Liv groans.

13

SHE HEARS THE KNOCK and burrows deeper under the sheets, palms pressed over her ears. She dreamed about awful things all night, she can't remember what, probably sharks. Her father didn't drown her at birth, so now he'll just feed her to the sharks. In *Jaws*, that shark mouth came right up out of the water and bit the boat in half!

"Liv, get up. Right now."

"I'm coming," she mutters.

"What?"

"I said, I'm getting up!"

She sits up, runs her tongue over her furry teeth. She feels like she's slept all of an hour. Her eyeballs are scratchy and she can feel herself working on a headache. She's probably catching the flu. He'll make her go anyway, there's no point in telling him.

Gran would have stuck a thermometer in Liv's mouth without her having to say anything. Liv would stay home from school, and they'd read poetry, curled up together on Gran's big bed. "Listen to this one, Gran!" And Gran would always close her eyes so that she could listen better.

The shower is running. Why would her father take a shower before going out and jumping in the ocean? If he was going to Sam's, then maybe, but just to go diving?

In the dark she feels around for the jeans she wore the day before. At the back of her closet a pair of running shoes waiting to start up again. Before she left the East Coast, she was jogging five miles through Central Park. She could start running on the beach. People around here do that, she's seen them. How is she going to get any exercise sitting on a boat all day?

He's out of the shower, dressed and waiting, as she heads into the bathroom.

"Don't take all day in there," he says. "You don't need to fix your face. You're going out on a boat—you're not going dancing!"

But she *has* to do her eyes.

When she's out: "Got a jacket?"

"Just my leather one."

He makes a face. "Well, that won't work. Spinuchi's left one on the boat. You can wear that. But bring a sweater, just in case." Her black cashmere sweater was a birthday gift from Gran. She ties it around her waist. Its warmth and softness lend her courage.

Out to the truck. No lights on anywhere. The cool predawn air raises goose bumps on her arms.

On the freeway he drives only as far as the next exit and turns off. There, in brilliant yellow and red, an open-all-night McDonald's. "Three egg McMuffins," he says to the board with all the food pictures on it. "And two coffees. Milk and sugar."

"I don't eat Mc-anythings," Liv announces.

"You do now." He drives up to the window, pays, gets a folded bag and a coffee tray. "Come on, Liv. Don't be difficult." He pulls a wrapped sandwich out of the bag and hands it to her.

She watches him pour two creamers and all three packs of the sugar into his coffee cup. He stirs it vigorously with the plastic stirrer. She takes a sip of her coffee, steaming black.

He drives while polishing off two of the muffins in several bites. She nibbles at the edges of hers, then takes a real bite. Last night's dinner didn't go very far. Finishing her McMuffin, Liv actually wishes she had another.

The freeway is almost deserted. Along the side, motels, an occasional restaurant, a scattering of parked cars. The sun is just beginning to rise. The patchy brown mountains turn pink. For several minutes everything is pink: her father's face, his hands on the wheel, her hands. Then the sun creeps above the horizon, shining gold, and the pink light fades. In the warm pink glow of morning, Liv had almost felt happy. For the first time in weeks she remembers what it's like, anyway, to feel happy again.

But it doesn't last.

"You're going to have to get some clothes," her father says, turning into the harbor parking lot.

"Clothes?"

"For work," he says. "There's a thrift shop down there next to the liquor store, you've seen it. Get yourself some blue jeans and sweatshirts. Maybe a pair of work boots . . ."

"In the *thrift* store?" She's never been in a thrift store in her life. The thought of wearing somebody else's clothes makes her shudder.

"Well," he drawls, "you can always go to the Gap. If you've got the money."

She gives him a sour look he doesn't see.

He parks and they both get out. He leans into the bed of the pickup and grabs a plastic milk crate. Hauling it over the side, he drops it into her arms. Her knees nearly buckle with the weight. "Might have to change the fuel pump," he says to the metal parts inside the crate. "It's been acting up."

He grabs a second crate and takes off in the direction of the boats. She follows, already out of breath with the effort of carrying the heavy crate. The one he's got is lighter, she could bet on it.

He jerks his chin at somebody behind the windows of the Breakwater. A hand waves back. The little café is full of people and it's only six o'clock. Liv figures they're all fishermen. Who else would be dumb enough to get up so early?

She's nervous. The greasy egg sandwich has unsettled her stomach. She's been on a boat only once before, and that was a ferry in Long Island Sound. When they get to the *Jeannie T*, her father throws her a musty brown jacket. She holds it out, between two fingers. "Do I have to wear this?"

"Nope. You can freeze instead if you want. Your choice."

She frowns at the jacket. Poor Brian Spinuchi with his broken arm. She puts it on.

"But this you have to wear." He tosses her a bulky orange life vest.

Liv pulls the vest on over the jacket, fumbling with the buckles and straps. Her father checks her over, yanks on a strap until the vest hugs her like death. "Where do I sit?" she says as the engine starts up, rumbling the deck under the soles of her running shoes.

"Sit?" As if he doesn't understand the language she's speaking. He lifts a hatch in the deck and props it up with a broom handle. Then, with a look as intent as a detective's, he begins poking around inside. "Always better to know what's wrong *before* you go out," he says. At last he drops the hatch and takes the wheel.

Liv looks around, then goes to stand next to her father at the front, at what Spinuchi called the "pulpit," where the steering wheel is. Her father looks over his shoulder, backing the boat out of its slip. They chug slowly out into it, passing sleeping boats, passing Sam somewhere out there in all those boats. Sam, who probably didn't sleep a wink.

She wants to be able to tell her father about Sam. She wants not to hold it all alone. But she can't tell him; she promised.

Sam's just protecting him. Or maybe herself. Maybe she

106

knows, deep down, that he won't be there for her. A guy who ducks out on his own kid can't be counted on for much, Sam should know that.

"How come you and Sam aren't married?"

Her question catches him flat-footed, the way she intended it to. The wind blows the thin strands of hair back from his high forehead as the speed of the boat increases. They have left the harbor behind and are heading for the open ocean.

"Why?" he says, stalling.

"Well, you're over there all the time. On her boat . . ."

"How do you know that?" He frowns at her.

"Oh come *on*! I'm not a child."

"Could have fooled me!" He laughs, a short, chopping laugh.

"So why?"

"She doesn't care about being married," he says, "that's why. She's never been married."

"That doesn't mean she doesn't want to marry *you*."

"Yeah, well . . ."

He pushes forward on the accelerator and the engine screams. "Hang on," he says. The nose of the little boat lifts, the deck tilts, and suddenly they're bouncing over the water so fast Liv's eyes start to stream. She clings to the edge of the pulpit with both hands. "Do you have to go this fast?" she yells in his ear.

He doesn't answer, his eyes squinting at something ahead, something she can't see, that probably isn't even there.

The boat pounds through the swells, water shooting up

in arching sprays on both sides. Liv tries to keep her knees loose, but already they're tired and aching from the effort of holding her balance. The boat hits the water again and again with thunderous claps. Liv's teeth chatter. She bites her tongue, metallic taste of blood in her mouth.

"Calm," he yells. "Good day!"

"Yeah, right," she mutters, but of course he can't hear her.

Soon they've left the city behind. To the left, farther out than she'd thought they'd be, a string of dark islands, humped like the backs of huge gray whales. The sun sparkles on the crests of waves, wavelets, peaked all around. The sea is blackish-greenish-blue, not at all the way it looked from shore. And deep. She doesn't want to think about how deep it is, or what's down there swimming around, eating things.

A spray of cold seawater over the top of the pulpit and they're both completely soaked. Her father hardly blinks. The pounding goes on and on. Hours, it feels like. Just when she thinks she can't stand it another minute, he slows the boat until the deck is level and they're idling, the exhaust burbling behind, churning the water white.

"Watch on your side for a plastic milk jug with a black T on it," he says. "We probably won't find it, but I could have missed it the other day."

He's taken them closer to shore. Up from a narrow strip of gravelly beach, the land rises in a soft yellow-brown slope. It looks like pictures Liv's seen of South Africa. The air smells alive in a way she's never before experienced it, rich with sea life. It is entirely possible that she is breathing clean air for the first time in her entire life, a jarring thought.

His nose sharp as a retriever's, her father searches the water on the right side of the boat. Liv scans her side. Every curl of foam looks like a milk jug.

He cuts the engine. Over the side goes the anchor. "It's somewhere near here," he says.

"What?"

"The reef."

While she watches, her face growing warm, he climbs out of his jeans and raggedy blue T-shirt. Wearing only a baggy pair of bathing trunks, he starts shaking baby powder all over himself, smoothing it down his white, hairy legs, over his strong tanned arms. His stomach is flat, a washboard stomach. His chest has gray curly hairs on it. It makes her squirm to see him half-dressed, but he seems not to notice that she isn't Spinuchi.

"Get me my suit," he orders. He points to a lidded box. Out of it she pulls a black rubber jacket with the smell she hadn't been able to identify before, the smell that clings to him like cheap cologne.

"There's another piece," he says. She pulls out another thing made of the thick black rubber. "No, not that one. The Farmer John." She finds the piece with the jumper top and passes it over.

He yanks up one leg of the Farmer John, then the other, like a woman getting into a stiff girdle. Then he puts on the zippered jacket, snapping it under his crotch. The jacket's hood goes up over his head. When he turns, his face is a pinched red oval and he can't look right or left without moving his whole body. Last, he pulls on a pair of rubber socklike things. Then he pads over to an engine-thing (Spinuchi told her the name of it, but she's forgotten), pulls a cord several times until smoke goes up and the engine-thing starts to chug. "See this hose?" he says. It looks just like a garden hose, only black instead of green.

She nods.

"After I dive, you throw this behind me. In coils, okay?"

"Uh . . . yeah, okay."

"Then all you have to do is keep an eye on your end of it," he says. "When you feel a tug, start pulling me in. Pull the slack out of the hose until you feel me on the end. Then yank hard. Just like fishing. Got that?"

"Yeah, I guess . . ."

Swells roll under the boat and on into shore. He rides the deck with ease; she totters, nearly slips. He grabs her arm and rights her. "You can sit," he says. "Just hold on to that hose. And if the compressor quits, give the hose three tugs. Got that? Three hard tugs. But make sure you've got me on the other end."

"Is that why they call you Tug?"

"What?"

"Because of the hose, three tugs and all that."

"Huh? Oh, no."

"Why then?"

"Why what?"

She groans. "Why do they call you Tug?"

"Aw," he says, looking away, and for a moment she thinks he's not going to tell her. He looks embarrassed, or annoyed. She doesn't know which. "Shark got hold of my fin one time, that's all . . ."

"A shark? A white shark?"

"Yeah, a white."

"Jeez! What did you do?"

"Well, he tugged and I tugged back. He gave up first."

"And so they call you—"

"Tug," he says grimly. "You got it."

"Aren't you afraid down there? I mean, what if another one attacks you?"

"Comes with the work," he says.

He shows her how to start the compressor. "Just like a lawnmower," he says, yanking a cord that turns a wheel on the side of the thing. "Ever mow a lawn?"

"Nope."

"Didn't think so," he says, with a rueful shake of his head, as if mowing lawns were some kind of *requirement* for living!

He puts on a belt hung with heavy chunks of metal, then his mask, and sticks the mouthpiece attached to the hose in his mouth. He huffs several times into the mouthpiece, pulls it out, and says, "Always check it first, *before* you hit the water!" as if she's about to dive in, too.

She waits for him to do a back flip into the water, like she's seen on Jacques Cousteau, but to her disappointment, he just pulls on his fins, climbs unceremoniously over the side, and slips in.

Pulling out his mouthpiece: "If you need to pee, just hang your butt over the side. No one will see you."

He plugs his mouth again and, with a quick, almost imperceptible kick, disappears into the dark water.

She stands. A panicky feeling washes over her. She is alone. Nobody to call, nobody to rescue her if she should, like, fall off the boat or something. In fact, she's got to watch out for *him*.

She holds on to the hose with both hands. It feels as if there's nothing on the other end, as if it's just dangling in the water. What if something's already happened to him and she didn't feel him tugging? The deck rides up and goes down, meeting the horizon and falling away. Her stomach goes with it. If she keeps her face to the wind, she feels okay. She takes a deep breath, several more, filling her lungs. Behind her, the smoke and fumes from the compressor.

The hose lies across the knees of her black jeans, which are already wet and dirty. The collar of Spinuchi's jacket is rough on her neck and fishy-smelling, which makes her stomach uneasy. She starts to get warm and a little sleepy. And the bile rises in her stomach. She makes a dive for the side, hangs her head over, and throws up until there's nothing left but green stringy stuff.

When she can pull herself back up, she sits shakily on her crate, the hose across her lap. She's never felt so sick in her life. It's worse than the flu, and there's no way to get out of it. Nowhere to go. Over the side again with dry heaves, holding the hose at the same time. If he dies down there, it's her fault.

She lays her forehead on the side of the boat, closes her eyes.

"Hey!" Her father's goggled face swims into her vision. "You sick?"

She closes her eyes again.

"Sit up," he orders. "Sit up and keep your eyes on the horizon."

She hauls herself up. He swims to the end of the boat. Holding his fins in one hand, he puts one foot on the outdrive. "Help me in," he orders, holding out his free hand. She pulls with everything she has. "You gotta help," he complains, stepping onto the deck.

He peels his hood off. "Nothing down there," he grumbles. "It's not the right place. I could've sworn . . ."

He pads over to the pulpit and starts the engine. "Pull the anchor."

She can hardly move without sending her stomach into spasms. Holding herself together, she begins to pull on the rope with her free hand.

Impatiently he grabs the rope and pulls the anchor in. Then he guns the engine, sending her sprawling onto the deck, where she hangs on for all she's worth as the *Jeannie T* bangs her way up the coast.

He dives a second time. This time Liv keeps her eyes on the horizon, and after a while her stomach settles some. The

Jeannie T bobs gently in a forest of huge reddish-brown leaves. Leaning over the side, she grabs one. It's slimy, attached to a hose-like stem. The water is clearer here. She can see where the brown stems go down and down.

A sharp tug on the hose surprises her. She begins to pull. She pulls until she feels his weight on the other end. The pulling gets harder then. Her shoulders ache by the time she sees him surface.

He yanks out his mouthpiece. "Here, grab this," he says. She sticks her fingers through the holes in the rope bag and tries to haul it over the side, but it won't come. She hangs on to it while he clambers in. With one hand, he hoists the bag over the side. "You've got to pull," he says. "Put your weight into it."

Inside the bag are six abalones and a fish. "Check them for size," he says, handing her his abalone iron. "They've got to come to here," he says, pointing to a tine on the iron, "or they go back. Don't cheat. The fish pigs will yank my license."

She measures each of the abalones carefully, fitting them between the tines on the iron he used to pry them free. If they are a fraction of an inch shorter than that space, they have to go back. He has to *take* them back, because that's the law. They have to be placed exactly where they were.

"That wasn't the reef," he says, frowning at his small catch.

The fish flips around the deck, gills heaving, glassy eyes staring.

114

Her father goes into the cabin and comes out with a bag of rolls, a jar of something that looks like bloody cabbage, a bottle of water, and some chocolate-chip cookies. He snatches up the fish, which can barely flip its tail now, and runs his knife down the middle of it, splitting it open. Liv looks away, at the horizon. Keeps her eyes there.

"Here, have some of this. It's calico bass. Best sushi in the world." A chunk of bluish-white fish dangles wetly at the end of his knife.

"No, thank you," she says.

"You don't eat sushi?"

"Well, yeah. In a *restaurant*!"

"Where do you think the restaurants get it, Liv?" The teasing look back in his eyes. "But your sushi came from New York, right? Ah, that's different! They probably fished it out of the stinking New York Harbor." He shakes his head. "Here, have some of this, then." He hands her the jar of bloody cabbage.

"What's this?"

"Kimchi. Korean. Good for what ails you."

She opens the jar and smells it, makes a face, screws the lid back on. She chews on a roll, watching him down the raw fish, chasing it with the kimchi and water.

"So," he says, wiping his mouth with the back of his hand, "another couple of dives and we'll call it a day. Unless I find that reef . . ."

He stands up, belches.

"You're not going in now, are you?"

"Might as well," he says.

"But you're not supposed to. You have to wait half an hour."

"Old wives' tale," he says, pulling his hood back on. And then he's gone again, the hose slipping through her hands, which are red and raw-looking.

Gloves. Tenders probably wear gloves, but he didn't think to tell her that. She'd have to get some gloves.

What is she thinking? This is her first, and *last*, day as an abalone tender. She'd beg Sam to give her a job at Shear Magic. Anything but *this*.

She gazes out at the hills, at three tall trees clustered in a graceful sort of circle, like ballerinas dancing with their arms up. She'd sketch those if she had her journal. Next time she'll bring—

But there isn't going to *be* a next time.

She is beginning to relax with the roll of the swells beneath the boat, giving in to them, riding them. She's learned this little lesson: not to fight so hard, to ride it out easy.

Something pops up in the water, a brown snout with whiskers, a seal's nose. The seal is watching her with liquid brown eyes, like a dog's. She laughs aloud and it disappears.

A tug on the hose and she begins hauling her father in again. "I saw a seal!" she says, pulling on his arm in her excitement.

"Sea lion," he says, stepping onto the deck. "There he is over there."

She turns, and there's the little brown snout again, and the curious eyes.

"You didn't find anything?"

"Nope."

He cranks up the engine. "One more spot I want to try," he says, and they're off again, tearing and banging across the water.

When he finds his spot—which looks exactly like every other spot in the ocean to her—he slows the boat and cuts the engine. "This might be it," he says. "The marker is gone, but this might be it."

The sky is a clear pale blue, and the sea sparkles with diamonds. When he's gone, Liv takes off the life vest and Spinuchi's jacket. She stands up and stretches, letting go of her hose for only that long. The warmth of the sun is healing to her tired shoulders and arms. She'd take a nap if she could. If she didn't have to tend the damned hose.

She puts the vest back on, certain of a lecture if she doesn't.

How strange to have your own father swimming around underneath you, attached to the end of a garden hose— well, it *looks* like a garden hose.

Really, and this is a weird thought, the hose is his umbilical cord. He's helpless as a baby down there in his world of water. He depends on that hose for his life—on *her*! for his life.

It seems forever before she feels the tug on the hose. This time she can hardly pull him in. The muscles in her arms and shoulders scream for her to stop, to let go, but she pulls and pulls, hand over hand. She's sweating and exhausted. Somehow he's gotten a lot heavier.

He pops up, yanks off his mouthpiece. "Found it!" She reaches for the bag that he pushes up to her. It's filled with abalone, and so heavy she can barely hold on to it with both hands. "If you drop that bag, you're going down after it," he says, but she can hear in his voice that he's happy. He's found his damned reef, and now he's happy.

14

ON THE WAY BACK DOWN THE COAST, Liv pulls Spinuchi's big jacket, fishy, musty, over her head and curls up into a ball at the back of the boat. Clamping her teeth together, she closes her eyes and takes the pounding of the *Jeannie T* in her stomach, her empty, hollow stomach. Up front, steering one-handed, her father rides the bucking boat as if he's glued to the deck. His hair wings back over his ears.

At last the engine slows and the deck levels out. Liv sticks her head up and sees that they're heading into the harbor. Overhead, a gull cries. She looks up and sees a dozen gulls gliding above the boat, holding the air without seeming to try. They are beautiful birds, soft gray and white or speckled brown, the younger ones that fly behind, but her father hates them all. Calls them "winged rats." They're only scavengers, though; it's how they live.

As they idle up to the loading dock, there are gulls everywhere, and pelicans, too, huge and prehistoric-looking, strolling around the dock or hunched down into their necks, keen golden eyes taking everything in, waiting for a handout.

The *Jeannie T* bumps against the pilings, and Liv's father tells her to throw a line up. She makes it on the second try.

"What'cha got there, Tug? Couple dozen snots?" The man who has grabbed the rope wears a blue knit cap pulled down to his eyes. A gray beard covers the rest of his face. He sends down a box that hangs by a steel cable from a winch.

"Almost three dozen. Thirty-two legals."

Liv helps her father pile the abs into the box.

"Musta hit a reef, huh? Where did you go? Smuggler's?"

"Nah, nah," her father says, backing the boat away. "Just up the coast."

"Ah! The Ranch . . ." the man says, but her father doesn't answer.

"Corky's got a big mouth," her father explains as they cross to Marina 1. "In half an hour it'll be all over the place that I hit the mother lode."

"Did you?"

"Did I what?"

"Hit the mother lode?"

"Maybe," he says. "But you gotta keep your mouth shut."

"Who am I going to tell? Sam?"

"I'm just saying—"

"Don't worry, I'm not going to tell anybody about your snots." She giggles, can't help it.

"Go on up to the Dory," her father says when the *Jeannie T* has been refueled and is once again in her berth. "I'll take a shower and be up in a bit."

Liv would like to take a shower, too, but she's got nothing clean to change into. Her jeans are covered with dried yuck—she knows now why they call the abalone "snots"— and so are her running shoes. Her hair has dried, but it's stiff with salt.

"You need to use the head?" he says.

"Yeah, I could wash up."

He gives her a look. "Yeah, you could," he says.

She follows him to the bathrooms. With his card he lets her into the women's. The mirror confirms her worst fears. What's left of her black mascara is smeared like ink in long streaks down her face. There's a smudge of dark lipstick along her jaw, but none at all on her pale lips. Night of the Living Dead. She stares at what's left of herself through eyes, her father's eyes, almost too exhausted to care. With a rough paper towel and the liquid soap, she washes the traces of makeup and saltwater from her face, runs her fingers through her stiff hair. She looks as if she's ready for bed. It's the only time she's this . . . naked.

She heads for the Dory, weak with hunger. If she's lucky, nobody will be there, nobody she knows. Not that she knows anybody.

A flash of white on the balcony. Then a hand goes up, waves. Spinuchi, Brian Spinuchi with his right arm in a white cast. Her heart sinks. She can't go up there now, not looking like this. She waves back, then ducks into the Coast Chandlery to watch for her father, head him off before he goes upstairs.

The Chandlery is filled with boat stuff, things to buy for boats, to wear when you're on a boat. Yellow rain slickers, boots. But she doesn't think this is what her father has in mind for her. What she needs is in the thrift store, somebody else's worn-out jeans.

Maybe he just took her out today to teach her a lesson, because he was pissed about the money. Maybe he'll find somebody else now, a guy.

She sees her father coming, stops him outside the shop. "Why don't we just, like, get a pizza or something," she says.

"Huh?" He looks at her face, her naked face, in the strangest way, his eyes dark and haunted-looking.

"What's the matter?" A hand goes up, covers her mouth and nose.

"Nothing," he says. "Nothing's the matter." But he can't seem to take his eyes off her.

"Yeah, I know. I look terrible, right?"

"No," he says quietly. "No, you don't look terrible. You look . . . fine."

And then it's too late to escape, because Spinuchi is coming toward them. Liv turns quickly away, as if she's looking for somebody, Sam maybe.

"Hey, guys!" says Spinuchi, his right arm across his chest, cradled in a sling. He's wearing his usual grin, as if nothing at all has happened to him. But when Liv turns around, his grin fades. In its place is a look Liv can't read. "Hey," he says again, this time more softly.

"Hey," she says. She can feel the heat in her face.

"Well, come on," says her father. "I thought you said you were hungry."

They troop up the stairs, Liv with her head down.

Inside the restaurant somebody is singing along with the jukebox. It's the respect song, that old Aretha Franklin thing. "R-E-S . . . !" Only it's badly off-key.

"Sam's been putting down a few," says Spinuchi with a grin.

Liv's father stops just inside the dining room. He gives Spinuchi his Tin Man look. "A few?"

"Yeah," Spinuchi says. "A few beers."

"But who's counting, right?" her father says.

Liv and Spinuchi follow him to the back of the dining room. Sam is swirling around on the last bar stool. "R-E-S-P-E-C-T! Tell me what you mean to me!" She sings in a kind of screeching croon, drowning out Aretha, which isn't easy. "A little respect now, yeah, yeah!" Sam breaks off when she sees them. "Well, there's my man now!" She slides off the bar stool, half falling against Liv's father, who grabs her arm, rights her the way he righted Liv on deck.

"What are you doing?" he says quietly, his eyes dark and intense, but puzzled, too, as if he really doesn't know.

"Hey, swee'pea!" slurs Sam. The smile she gives Liv is

wobbly. "Did you have fun today?" Then she pulls her head back like a fish into a cave and squints. "Hey, you're a pretty girl, you know that? She's a doll! Isn't she, Mark?"

Her father says nothing. He waits. He waits like a rock.

"And poor Spinach! Whoops." She reaches up and covers her grin. "I mean Spinuchi! How's your arm, baby?"

"Let's go, Sam," her father says in that same patient, quiet voice.

"Go? I'm jus' gettin' started, honey man! Come on, have a beer with me."

"You've had enough," he says.

"Aw, Mark, you old killjoy. You just don't know how to have fun. You know that?" She pats his expressionless face. "Your daddy?" she says, turning to Liv, clutching Liv's arm, steadying herself. "Your daddy is one—"

"That's enough," he says. "We're going now."

"I'll go when I'm good and ready," Sam says, suddenly sounding sober. "And I'm not good and ready yet." She pulls herself onto the bar stool and orders another beer. "With a whiskey back," she says, looking straight at Liv's father, daring him to stop her.

Her father sighs. "You two go ahead and have some chowder," he says to Liv and Spinuchi. "Tell them to give me the bill." He slides onto the stool next to Sam. She slings an arm around him, leans her curly head against his shoulder.

Liv and Spinuchi take a table outside on the balcony.

"Man, is she loaded!" chuckles Spinuchi. He glances behind him, through the window at the bar.

"Well, my father will put her fire out, that's for sure," says Liv. "Sam's right. He's a—what did she call him?"

"A killjoy." His grin fades. "She's supposed to be on the wagon. Anyway, that's what he told me."

A waitress comes out. Spinuchi asks for the chowder, so Liv does, too. "And fries," she says. "A double order."

"Hungry, huh?"

"Starved!"

He laughs, shakes his head, knowing that kind of hunger. "So how was it, working for your dad?"

Liv catches herself before she says what really isn't true. It wasn't "awful." It was hard work, and sometimes she was afraid, but that was only until her father explained things, then she was fine. "It was okay," she says. "I saw a seal. A sea lion."

"No sharks?"

"No sharks."

"Wait till you see the dolphins, they're amazing! It's like being at Sea World!" He laughs at himself. "Well, better."

"Then I guess I'll go to Sea World to see them. How long until you can work again?"

"Six weeks, the doctor says. Think you can hang on that long?"

"Me? Oh, no. He's got to find somebody else. Anyhow, I wasn't much good out there. I could hardly pull him in!"

"The main thing is to make sure he's getting air. The rest he can really manage himself. Oh, he'll piss and moan, but he doesn't need anybody to pull him in. It just makes it easier."

The waitress comes with two wide bowls of thick red chowder and a basket of sourdough bread. "Your fries will be out in a sec," she says.

Liv dives in. They slurp their soup in silence, Spinuchi awkward with his left hand.

"Want me to butter you some bread?"

"Hey, yeah. Thanks," he says, and gives her that wide sweet grin again. He glances over the rail, nods. "Look, there they go."

Liv looks down, sees Sam and her father walking arm in arm in the direction of Sam's boat. Then she sees they're not exactly arm in arm, it's more like he's holding her up. Liv's hoping Sam will tell him now, that it'll just slip out about the operation. Then Liv won't have to keep the secret anymore.

"I almost didn't recognize you when you came up from the boat," says Spinuchi, swiping his bread in the remains of his chowder. "I was looking for, you know, the girl I met before."

"Huh?"

"Well, I mean you look different today, without all the, without . . ."

She decides to save him. "Makeup. Without all the makeup."

He grins. "Yeah."

"Well, it all washed off!"

"You look fine without it. I mean—" His eyes widen.

She can tell he doesn't want to hurt her feelings, but she

decides not to save him this time. "So I don't look 'fine' with it? Is that what you mean?"

"What? No! I mean, you look . . . okay either way! Aw heck, what I mean is—"

She laughs. "Never mind. I know what you mean. It's okay. Really." But it isn't. He's been looking at her differently today, and it's hard not to like that.

15

LIV UNPACKS TWO PBJs and a carton of lemonade and sets them on the seawall between herself and Sam. It's an overcast day, almost cold. Her father is working on somebody's engine, so Liv has the day free.

Sam said little on the walk over from Shear Magic, and Liv, not knowing what to say about yesterday—anything? should she say anything?—was quiet, too. If it had been Megan walking beside her, she'd have given her a bad time, but she'd probably be joking, too. If it were Suds—but it wouldn't be Suds. Suds didn't drink. Sam is a friend, but she's also her father's girlfriend. And she's an adult. Adults were supposed to know what they were doing, and if they screwed up, they sure as heck didn't want to hear about it.

Sam picks up her sandwich and puts it down again. "I'm sorry, sweetie. I can't eat. My stomach's a mess."

"Oh."

Sam starts to say something and stops. She sighs. "Not exactly a role model, am I?"

Liv rubs at a scratch on the back of her hand. "I don't know . . ."

"Sure you do. Don't give me that garbage, Liv. I fell off the wagon. Hard. Haven't had a drink in six years. Until yesterday, when I tried making up for it all in one day." She shakes her head ruefully. "I'm scared, honey. That's the truth. I remember my mom, how it was for her . . ."

Liv bites her lip. She's scared, too, but Sam doesn't need to hear that. "Did you tell him? Did you tell my father? Last night?"

"Nope." Sam flicks a piece of tobacco off the hem of her short white skirt.

"I think you should tell him," Liv says. What she doesn't say is that she doesn't want to have Sam's secret anymore. She doesn't want to worry about Sam all by herself.

Sam looks up over the top of her sunglasses. "Oh, you do, huh? Aren't you the one who said he'd probably cut out on me?"

Liv sighs. "Something like that. But what do I know? I don't even know him!"

Sam frowns, stares down at her bare freckled knees. "Well, I think you're probably right. I've never tested him, and I'm not sure I want to now."

Liv blurts, "Well, what good is he if he just—if he *cuts out*?"

Sam smiles a faraway smile. "You got a point, kid," she says.

Liv and Sam stop at the thrift store on the way back to Shear Magic. Sam makes such a fun game of the shopping, waving 38 Triple D cup bras with their sprung elastic, prancing around in a spangled boa and silver cowboy boots, that Liv forgets that all the clothes are castoffs. She is standing at the counter, letting Sam pay for two pairs of men's faded jeans and a pair of work boots, when it hits her. She's going to go out to sea with her father again. Why else would they be buying all this stuff?

Well, she doesn't exactly have a choice. She owes him. Wait till he sees the phone bill! But it comes as a surprise that a part of her, maybe a big part, really wants to go.

So it surprises her even more when he says that tomorrow, and "maybe a couple of days," he's going out alone.

"How come? I did a good job, didn't I?"

He's just come in, covered with grease, smelling like a garage. He avoids her eyes.

She pushes harder. "Well, you didn't say I did a bad job, right?"

"You did okay," he concedes. "It's got nothing to do with you."

"Then what? You're not supposed to go out alone!"

"Who says?"

"Oh come on. Sam says, *everybody* says."

"Yeah, well, everybody's full of crap." He goes into the bathroom, closes the door.

She talks to the door. "Are you mad at Sam? Is that what's wrong? Because she got drunk?"

He opens the door, looks straight at her as if he's surprised to find her there. "No, I'm not mad at anybody. I'm just going out to the islands for a couple days. Sam will stay here with you."

"I don't need anybody to stay with me. I'm not exactly a child."

"Not *exactly*." Anybody else would be grinning. Not him. He bends over his box of clothes, shifting things in neat piles, looking for what he needs.

"When did you see Sam?"

"Just now. Why?" He turns, a towel and clean shirt over one arm.

"Well, what did she say?"

He gives her a look that bores through her like a drill. "Nothing. She said she'd stay with you, that's all. There's money in the box."

"Well, *fine*. Go by yourself, what do I care?" Liv turns away, stalks across the brown rug, slams into her room. She hears him leave. The tiny chink in the Tin Man's armor has sealed itself over. For a while on the boat they were almost easy together. Now he's back to who he really is.

She hates him. She hates her father.

Liv hears him leave in the morning, tries to pretend she doesn't care that he's left her behind. But she does.

After work Sam shows up at the door with a duffel bag and a bucket of chicken. "Extra crispy," she says. Her hair is stuck on top of her head and pinned with a black-and-white polka-dot bow. Her earrings look like fishing lures. "I hope that's all right."

"You don't have to babysit me, Sam."

"I know, toots. Your father doesn't know, but I do. I just thought you'd like the company. And some chicken." She sets the bucket on the table, her overnight bag in his chair.

Liv's been talking to herself and her father since he went out the door, and now she's fuming. "He's such a big fat jerk!" She throws up her hands.

"Well, not so fat!" laughs Sam.

"But he *is* a jerk! He just wants us to worry about him. That's why he's going out alone! He tells me to get myself some work clothes, and then what does he do?" Liv paces the spotted brown carpet. "Goes without me."

Sam slumps into the couch, lays her head back, closes her eyes. "I told him," she sighs, "about the surgery."

"Oh." Liv comes to a dead stop in front of the couch.

Sam opens her eyes, sits up. She leans her elbows on her knees, sticks her chin in the palms of her hands. "And you're right. He took off." Slow shake of her head, as if she still can't quite believe it. "He'll be back, but . . . not really."

Liv drops to the floor, folds her legs in. "What do you mean?"

"I mean, he won't be there for me. He can't."

"Can't? *Can't?* That's *lame!*"

Sam considers. "Maybe." She looks straight at Liv now. "How much do you know about your mom and dad, Liv?"

Liv considers. "Not much. I mean, I know what Gran told me . . ." It's never occurred to her that Gran wouldn't tell her everything. She told her about the bad hearts—the congenital heart disease—and that she, Liv, was fine. Somehow she got lucky and the bad hearts skipped her.

Sam lights two cigarettes at the same time, passes one to Liv. "Well, they were young, your dad and mom. I guess you know that. Your mom was *really* young, only sixteen when they met."

"Yeah, I know."

"And she had this . . . this heart problem. I guess you knew that, too."

"Well, sure. That's what"—Liv looks down at her reddened hands—"that's why she died." She doesn't add that it's always seemed to be *her* fault. If she hadn't been born, Jean Trager might still be alive.

Sam says nothing for a few minutes. She glances around for a place to dump her cigarette ash. Finally, she flicks it into an abalone shell, one of the stack between the couch and the chair that Liv's father picks at hour after hour. "Your father blames himself for that, honey. He really believes he killed her."

"But that's . . . stupid! She died because of her heart . . . because she had a heart defect."

"Yeah, well, he knew that, you see. Your father knew she had a bad heart, that she should never have had children."

"And they . . . *he* . . . did it anyway." Liv sees in her mind a young boy and girl who are supposed to be her parents. It's hard to own them, but it hurts just the same.

"Well, he tried not to get her pregnant, but . . . Well, obviously it didn't work." Sam half-smiles at Liv, wanting her to understand, as if there's nothing else to be done and so she might as well try to understand. "He hates himself for that, Liv. When he talks about it . . . well, that one time when he did talk about it . . . it's like it happened yesterday."

Liv feels the tears slicking down her cheeks, dropping onto her T-shirt. Impatiently she brushes them away. Who is she crying for? The sixteen-year-old mother that she never knew? Herself? Not her father. He doesn't deserve her tears.

"And so, he *can't* stick around." Sam's grin is shaky. "I guess I knew it all along. He can't take the chance of getting slammed like that all over again."

Liv looks at Sam, at her eyes so full of concern for Liv and for Liv's father. "He doesn't deserve you, Sam."

"Deserve, schmerv." Sam laughs. "What's that got to do with anything? I love the big fat jerk."

They eat the entire bucket of chicken, wiping their greasy fingers with paper towels, swilling down root beer. "I almost got us a movie," Sam says, "but then I remembered that your dad doesn't have a VCR."

"Or anything else!" Liv scans the entire apartment in a single glance. "This place is such a dump!"

"Hey, I know how to fix him," Sam says, as if a light's gone on over her head.

"Yeah?"

"We'll redecorate! Paint the walls pink! Buy lamps with ruffled shades."

"A picture on the wall," Liv says, getting into it, "one of those ugly farm scenes with cows!"

"Lace doilies all over his chair!"

Liv is in stitches. "Wouldn't that be great?"

"No, I mean it, Liv! I'm off the next two days. We can paint this whole place in a couple of hours."

"Pink?"

"What do you have against pink?"

"Nothing, only—" From brown to pink didn't seem like an improvement.

"Well, maybe not pink. Peach. And yellow in the kitchen, butter yellow."

Liv glances around, imagining the transformation. And then she thinks about her father. "He won't even notice."

Sam's eyebrows go up. "If he doesn't drop his jaw, then we haven't done our job right."

"I don't know . . ." It sounds like fun, but what if her father just gets madder? She's the one who has to live with him. For now, anyway.

"Come on," says Sam, hopping up from the couch. "Let's go into town, see a movie, have a hot fudge sundae or something. We gotta get our strength up, girl! We've got a big day ahead of us."

16

LIV GETS UP EARLY, tiptoes past the sleeping Sam. She muffles the grinder against her chest to deaden the sound and makes a pot of coffee. She dreamed about her father, about being in an underwater garden with her father, a garden with tulips, tomatoes, and goldfish. "Your grandmother is down here somewhere," her father said through his bubbles. "She's hiding." Liv awoke with a pounding heart.

"Mmmmm! Is that coffee I smell?" Sam, wearing her granny gown, drifts sleepily into the kitchen. "I dreamed about your dad," she says. "I know he'll be all right, he's been out lots of times by himself, but I guess I still worry."

"I dreamed about him, too!"

"Won't leave us alone, will he?" Sam laughs. "But we'll fix him." She sips her black coffee, sniffs the steam. "Oh, Liv! This is great!"

Liv grins. "I *told* you!"

• • •

At the paint store they mull over dozens of paint chips, from peachy-peach to almost white. They settle for one in the middle called "blush."

"It's perfect," Sam says, holding the chip at arm's length. "Now we need that buttery yellow." She searches through the yellow chips and pulls one out. "How about this?"

Liv squints at the chip. "That's not butter, that's mustard."

"Hmmm, maybe you're right." She skims a coral finger-nail along the chips and finds another. "How about . . . but-tercup?"

"Kind of bright," Liv says. Gran's walls were off-white, you didn't even notice them. "How about this one?" She holds up a chip called Sea Lavender. Peach and lavender, the sky above the harbor in the morning.

"Well, if that's what you want," says Sam doubtfully.

"Won't the manager get mad if we just go ahead and paint whatever color we want?"

"All she cares about is the rent," says Sam. "The owner lives in Singapore."

By late afternoon they've hauled the furniture into the parking lot and painted the living room. With the drapes down, Liv is amazed at how different the place looks, full of light, almost pretty.

"It's a shame to put those old drapes back up," Sam muses. There's paint in her hair, all over her hands and her freckled arms. Liv has been more careful, but she, too, is splattered with peach-colored freckles. They've been painting for hours, listening to the oldies station, Sam singing off-key along with the songs. "Oh, I love this one!" she'd cry, or: "This is the song I made out to the very first time!" And she'd sing at the top of her lungs, trying to dance and paint at the same time. "Let's hit the thrift store again. Maybe we can find some drapes."

But after dinner, pepperoni and pineapple pizza delivered to the door, they each fall asleep on opposite sides of the couch, exhausted.

The next morning they paint the kitchen. When they've finished, Liv steps back to evaluate. "It's gorgeous," she says.

Sam slings an arm over Liv's shoulders. "Too bad about those cupboards, though. We could paint them, too. Bright blue, maybe."

Liv looks at Sam to see if she's serious. She is. "Maybe some other time . . ." Liv says.

In the afternoon they go back to the thrift shop. Liv picks through a rack of sheets and curtains and tablecloths, while Sam goes off in search of pictures for the newly painted walls. Liv finds some off-white drapes. They're a little ragged on the bottom, but they're clean and look long enough. She's pulling them off the rack to get a better look when she gets one of those strange off-balance feelings: What is she doing? Where is she? *Who* is she? How can it be that in just a few weeks her life is so completely different? Upside down. And will it change again? What if Sam is really sick, like *dying*? Could Liv stand to live here without Sam? She holds the drapes, but she isn't really seeing them, she's thinking about Sam, about how close she feels to her, how dumb that is. But Sam doesn't allow anything else. It's impossible not to love Sam.

"Will you look at this!" Sam comes back hauling a huge painting. She turns it around so that Liv can see.

"Cows!" shrieks Liv. It's one of those strange paintings with fat naked women and men dressed in three-piece suits. They're all sitting in a pasture having a picnic. Right in the front, as if they're the most important thing, black-and-white cows graze on pea-green grass. "It's horrible! It's perfect!"

"I knew you'd like it," says Sam with a wide grin, on the verge of breaking up.

They leave the shop, their arms filled with purchases: a multicolored crocheted throw for the couch; the drapes and the painting; for the kitchen, ruffled curtains with old-fashioned coffeepots on them; for the living room a shaggy throw rug that looks like Beethoven, the movie dog, and an ashtray from the Stardust Hotel in Las Vegas. "We'll hide this," Sam says.

When everything is in place, they celebrate with sparkling cider. "We should have bought champagne glasses," says Liv.

"Next time," says Sam, clinking her water glass against Liv's coffee cup. "Here's to . . . well, lots of next times!" She holds up her glass for a toast. "Good times!"

"Here's to you, Sam," says Liv, thinking they won't all be good times. She can't say anything else without choking up.

"I'll drink to that," says Sam, downing her cider.

"When do you think my father will be home?" Liv can't wait to see his reaction to all this. If there *is* one. And then she realizes that it doesn't really matter what he thinks, that *she* likes it. It's funky, it's part Sam and part Liv. The next time she goes to the thrift store, she'll look for a bookcase. For her one poetry book. But there will be other books. Gran always said a house wasn't a home without books.

"You would have loved my Gran," Liv says.

Sam is scraping a splotch of paint off the top of the TV with her fingernail. "Well, if she was anything like you, I would have."

"She was great," Liv says sadly. "She was funny and smart, and well, she just was a very strong person."

"I'm sure she was."

"That's why I know you would have liked her. She was a lot like you."

"*Moi?*" Sam's coral fingertips splayed over her chest.

Liv's managed to embarrass them both, but it doesn't matter, not really. "Yeah, you," she says.

"You know," Sam says, as if she's really been thinking hard, "if I do have the big C, I mean if it's really bad and all, I'm going to buy me a new car!"

"Oh, Sam, how can you kid about a thing like that!"

Raised eyebrows, wide green eyes. "You think I'm kidding?"

They're sharing sweet-and-sour pork and fried rice when Liv hears the truck. "Oh my God. It's him!"

"Settle down, settle down. We'll just pretend nothing's happened. Like the good fairies came and did it all when we were sleeping."

They keep their eyes fixed on each other's faces, trying desperately not to crack up.

The door opens. The door closes.

"Huh."

Sam clamps a hand over her mouth, Liv bites her tongue.

The door opens and closes again. They both turn. He's gone.

"What the heck . . . ?" says Sam, and starts to get up.

Then he comes in again. "Thought I had the wrong place," he says. It's as close as he can come to a joke, and he expects them to laugh.

"Welcome to *Chez* Hope!" cries Sam, throwing her arms around him. "How do you like it?"

He frowns, walks the length of the room, stops in front of the painting, peers at it frowning. "Cows," he says.

"Cows!" cries Liv, and cracks up. She falls onto the couch, clutching her stomach. Tears roll down her face, she can hardly get a breath. "Cows!"

Then Sam is laughing, too. Liv's father looks at them both as if they've lost their minds and need to be hauled away. "Who did all this? You two?"

"Who else," cries Liv. "Ralph Lauren?"

"Ralph who?" Then to Sam: "Should you be . . . you know. Moving furniture and all that?" He looks uncomfortable, but holds the center of the room in his usual demanding way.

"Me?" asks Sam. "Sure, why not? I'm not pregnant!"

"Huh," Liv's father says. He looks as if he knows he should say something more, but he doesn't seem to know what that might be. "Well, it looks . . . nice," he says. "Maybe we could get some new furniture. Sometime."

"Oh, we love this couch. Don't we, Liv?"

"We do?" says Liv, and all three laugh, even her father.

"Got any more of that greasy Chink food?" he says.

"Mark!"

"*What?* What did I do now?"

Between bites, he tells them about the diving. The weather was good and the diving was easy, but he got only a dozen and a half, hardly worth the trip. "We'll go back up to the Ranch tomorrow," he tells Liv.

"I got some work clothes," says Liv, excited. "Some boots."

"That's good," he says. "I suppose you spent all the money. On the clothes and all the"—he glances around the apartment—"all the stuff."

"Ralph Lauren doesn't come cheap," she says, straight-faced.

She looks over at Sam. Sam's eyes are on her father, and in those eyes so many things, so much expectation and, well, fear maybe, that Liv glances away. It hurts too much to look.

17

HE ALWAYS KNOCKS on her door at 4:30, but Liv is up before that knock now, thanks to Gran's travel clock and an excitement she doesn't want to admit. She commandeers the shower before he can get to it, takes her time with her makeup. Even so, looking at her outlined eyes and Black Beauty lips, she has to wonder why. Who's it for? Him? The fish? But leaving the bathroom, she feels put together, which is the point.

Into a plastic bag she puts her Walkman, Yeats, a couple of cigarettes, a giant-sized bag of M&Ms, and her journal.

This morning, while he's showering, she heats up a jar of "fresh" coffee, opens a box of glazed doughnuts for breakfast. The apartment still smells of fresh paint; the kitchen walls are the color of a cheap coffin. Maybe a better light in the ceiling would help. She'll see what there is at the thrift shop. She used to shop at Bloomies, Barney's. Now she's just a bag lady, a bag kid. But her new-old jeans cling softly to her hips, as if they've always been hers. Over her T-shirt she wears a plaid flannel shirt, men's size large. Her father doesn't seem to know the difference between her and his other worthless moron tenders.

How many times she's thought, If Gran could only see me now.

Memories of Gran weave in and out of Liv's mind easily, like the notes of a sad, sweet song. Sometimes they make her cry, but once she laughed out loud remembering Gran's last spring hat. It looked exactly like a flying saucer, a huge pea-green disk with black button "eyes." Instead of watching the parade, people would turn and stare at Gran. Children pointed, teens giggled. Liv was embarrassed for Gran, for herself, too.

But Gran was flushed and proud. "Well!" she beamed, as she took the hat off and put it in its special box. "Didn't I cause a fuss, though! That's what a good hat will do, Liv," she said, with a shake of her finger. "Never forget it!"

This morning they've beat the sun. As they cruise out of the harbor, a golden inch of sunlight cracks the horizon. Liv watches transfixed as the sky changes almost by the second, from murky gray clouds to blue the color of Gran's delphiniums, then to wisps of lavender and rose. It's a deep serious blue by the time they reach the Ranch.

Her father slows the boat several times, looking at the land, then something farther up the coast, trying to get his bearings. "I think it was here," he says.

"You should have marked the spot," Liv says. "I told you."

"If I'd marked it, there'd be nothing down there," he says. "It'd be picked clean, believe me."

"But you *do*," she insists. "You do mark your spots. With milk cartons."

"Sometimes," he admits. "But you have to use landmarks. See that stretch of beach? The reef is somewhere between that and the point."

He cuts the engine at last. "This is it," he says, sending the anchor over the side.

"No, it isn't. We were closer to the three trees."

Ignoring her, he suits up, climbs over the side. She hands him his fins and he's gone.

The ocean is flat this morning, glassy. Black glass. On the surface lie thick reddish-brown kelp leaves. The *Jeannie T* is like a floating bathtub. Liv gets as comfortable as she can, leaning against the side of the boat, the black hose snaking across her legs.

She rips open the bag of M&Ms, pops a few. Then, up on her knees, she stares down into the dark water, down the brown stalks of kelp, wishing she could see something. Her father's hose in her right hand is still. He's down there somewhere, swimming around, seeing . . . what? There must be all kinds of stuff to see, but he doesn't say anything about it. He might as well be fixing elevators for a living.

And up he comes. He's a dark shape at first, then an astronaut in space, then her father. "Not here," he says, popping up.

"I told you," she says, helping him in.

They cruise slowly up the coast, the engine burbling behind, exhaust churning the water white. "Here!" she calls out. "Right here."

He turns and frowns. "Can't be."

"It is," she insists. "I'm sure of it."

To her surprise, he cuts the engine. She lets down the anchor, pulls to make sure it grabs. "Can't be," he says again, but he goes down anyway.

She reads some Yeats, puts on her Walkman, takes out her journal, writes several pages. The words come easily, with so much to talk about, so much that's different. Then she starts to sketch the three trees dancing. It reminds her of a Matisse painting Gran loved, dancers in a circle against a bright blue background. When she's finished, she holds the drawing at arm's length to appraise it. It's good, one of the best she's done. She wishes she could show it to Gran. All those pictures on the fridge over the years, that's why she likes to draw. Because Gran made her think she was an artist. She begins to draw a kelp leaf, which is really a lot more intricate than it looked at first. The boat bobs gently beneath her. She takes off her Walkman, stretches, gives her face to the sun, thinks about Sam. It is peaceful out here, and . . . *quiet!*

The compressor!

Liv leaps up. Her journal clatters to the deck, along with her Walkman. With hands shaking so badly she can hardly use them, she manages to wind the cord around the flywheel. She yanks it hard and the cord comes off in her hands. "Oh God, no!" She winds it again, pulls it again. Nothing. Helplessly she looks out onto the kelp-strewn water. Quiet. Dead quiet. No sound at all. No wind, no waves. Trembling, terrified, Liv winds the cord again. This time she yanks so hard she knocks herself off balance. With a loud chug and a plume of smoke, the compressor starts. Her legs gone to water, Liv sinks to the deck, the black hose in her hands, sick with fear. Is he all right? How long was the compressor off? She doesn't know, she was listening, like an idiot, to her music. She starts to pull on the hose. She pulls and pulls. Nothing's on the other end. And then there is. She tugs, he tugs back. She tugs again, harder. She waits. Finally, his hooded head pops up half a football field away. She's sick with relief, guilty relief. He swims in a leisurely crawl to the side of the boat. "What's going on?" he says, hanging by one hand to the side.

"The compressor!" she cries. "It quit!"

"Yeah? So?"

She stares at him in disbelief. "So? So didn't you run out of air?"

"Yeah, that's why I came up." He turns toward the compressor, listens. "It's running now."

"Well, yeah. I got it started again."

"So why did you pull on the hose?"

Exasperated, she throws up her hands. "To tell you about the compressor!"

"But it's working." He says the words slowly and patiently, as if she's dimwitted.

"Right," she says, giving up. "It's working."

He climbs into the boat, turns off the compressor. Liv quickly stuffs her Walkman into a pocket of Spinuchi's big jacket.

He goes into the cabin and comes out with lunch, the three tuna sandwiches she made the night before. She thought she'd please him, or at least surprise him this morning when she had everything ready. But he acted as if shopping for food and making his lunch were just another part of her job. Maybe they are, how would she know? But at least he's paying her. Ten percent of his catch: $40.00 so far.

He polishes off a sandwich in a half-dozen bites, reaches for another. "Can you swim?"

"Yeah, I can swim." Shouldn't he have asked her this before?

"Then I suppose you don't have to wear that life vest the whole time. At least, not when we're anchored. Where did you learn? The Y?"

"Yeah. What's wrong with that?"

"I didn't say there was anything *wrong* with that. I just asked where you learned to swim."

It's enough to kill the appetite, the way they talk to each other.

"Did you dive for pennies? Stuff like that?"

"Yeah." Liv got the silver dollar once, the biggest prize. She's a strong swimmer, built for it because of her broad shoulders, or so the coach said.

"Tell me about my mom," Liv says, surprising herself, surprising him even more. His eyes widen, then they get wary, defensive.

He crumples up the aluminum foil, makes a ball of it between his big square fingers. "Didn't your grandmother tell you about your mother?"

"Of course she did. I just want to know what *you* thought about her."

He wipes his mouth with a paper towel, shakes his head. "I married her, didn't I?"

"Well, duh . . . !"

His eyes get hard. "What is it you want to know, Liv? Was she like you? Do you look like her? Yes and no."

"How was she like me?" Her voice softer now, almost pleading.

He frowns at his sandwich. "She looked like you. A little. The way you looked the other day."

"Without the makeup," she says.

"But she wasn't as tall as you. And she didn't have your smart mouth."

"I guess I get that from you," she says.

He munches on a doughnut, his eyes somewhere over her right shoulder. He doesn't take the bait.

She pushes on. "Did you know her a long time before you two got married?"

He considers. "Three weeks."

"Three weeks!" she says incredulously. "How could you know—"

"You just know," he says. His jaw locks down whenever he's sure of something, which is all the time. "Anyway, *I* did." He slaps his big hands on his knees. "Okay, enough. Back to work." He stands.

"Dad?"

It hangs between them in the air, that single word. It's the first time she's called him Dad.

"Yeah?" The hood back on his head, his face pinched and red, he looms over.

"Did you guys ever, you know, talk about having, well, having me? Having a baby?" She's gone too far now, she knows that.

He stares down at her, his long arms loose at his sides. A gull passes overhead, keening. The *Jeannie T* dips and rises, gently, quietly, as if she were listening. Her father turns away.

Liv sighs. "You weren't in the right place," she says at last, passing him his fins. "It's over there." She points to the spot she remembers, straight out from the base of the middle tree. He disappears into the glassy water.

A swell has begun to build. Liv keeps her eyes on the line of the horizon. She watches a flock of birds, big birds, heading up the coast, flying close to the water, dipping and rising over the swells. Brown pelicans. And then, as if it's just for her, they perform an amazing aerial show. First one bird, then another, folds its huge wings and dives straight into the ocean, righting itself seconds later with barely a splash on the surface, swallowing its catch down its long, skinny neck. Splash, splash, splash. Like kamikazes at breakneck speed, heading straight for the water. Liv's laughing out loud, though there's not a soul around to hear her. Then a flock of seagulls appears out of nowhere, hanging around for bits of dropped fish. It's better than a circus.

The hose jerks, and hand over hand, Liv pulls her father in. "Found it!" he says, pushing up the rope bag so that she can catch on to it. It's full to bursting. "I knew it was around here somewhere." Not a word of acknowledgment that it was she who told him where to find his reef. Why does she keep expecting what he'll never give?

She measures the abalones, realizing as she does so that she has learned something: how to tell one kind of abalone from another, the reds from the pinks from the greens. What used to look like chunks of cement to her now have personality. Each one looks a little different, though they all have rough-ridged backs and barnacles stuck to them. As she lifts them from the bag, they suck their ruffled "feet" all the way up into their shells. They know something's not right, that their lives have been turned upside down.

The last one in the bag is bigger than all the rest, a granddaddy. "Can I have this shell?" she asks her father.

"Why not," he says. "We'll take that one for dinner."

And then she's sorry she asked.

"Well, maybe we should take a smaller one," she suggests.

"Doesn't matter," he says. "I get paid by the dozen, not the pound."

"Should I call Sam?"

He's got the skillet on the hot plate and the butter already in it, melting in a pool the color Sam wanted to paint the walls.

"Why?"

151

"She can come for dinner. I got stuff for a salad and some bread."

"Call her if you want," he mutters.

"Well, do you want me to?"

"It's up to you," he says, the laying of the abalone into the skillet taking all his attention.

She dials Sam's number. It rings and rings. "Not home," she says.

"Probably out tying one on," her father says.

She stares at him. How can anybody be so insensitive? It's almost as if he's trying to be as awful as he can be, as if he wants people to hate him. "That's not fair, Dad, and you know it. She slipped off the wagon, that's all. Once. One time. In six years!"

"Yeah, yeah, I know." He sounds tired.

"Do you know why she did that?"

He doesn't answer.

"Well, *do you?*" Her boldness jitters her insides. She expects him to get angry, defensive, but he doesn't. He's like one of those eels she saw on a nature show once, fierce at the opening of its cave, but ducking away to hide the minute you challenged it.

Moodily he pushes the abalone slices around the skillet. "She slipped. Just like you said. People slip all the time. There doesn't have to be a reason."

"Cancer's a pretty good reason," she says.

He flips the abalone, pushes it around so that each piece is exactly the same distance from the next. "She doesn't have cancer," he says.

"Oh, you *know* that," she scoffs, "you know everything!"

No answer. He slides the cooked abalone onto their plates. "I thought you said there was salad."

Sighing, she opens the fridge, takes out the lettuce, the tomatoes, the bottled dressing.

They eat in silence, only the sounds of the silverware tap-tapping on the plates. He gets up at last, washes his plate with a drizzle of soap, his hand cleaning the plate, both sides carefully as a surgeon. Then a shake of the plate, then the careful drying over and over, and the folding of the towel just so on the side of the sink. It makes her crazy to watch.

Finally, he goes into the living room and turns on the television. Liv stares at the lavender wall. Her shoulders and back ache with tiredness. She feels old and used up. She needs a cigarette.

"Where are you going?" he says.

"Just out here," she says. "Don't *worry*, I'm not running away from home."

She plunks down in a beach chair, lights up. It's the first she's had all day. Something about being out at sea doesn't go with a lung full of smoke. Maybe she'll just give it up. Cigs are too hard to get anyway, and she really can't afford to buy them. The pop-pop sound of TV gunfire comes from inside. Without seeing him, she knows her father is sitting in his chair, meticulously picking at his shells, and he'll be sleeping in no time, his head dropped to his chest, the bug sticker slack in his hand.

She doesn't dare take off for the beach. She's his prisoner.

No, she's his slave. He works her half to death because he owns her.

The door opens, and to her surprise, out he comes. He unfolds the other beach chair and sits down heavily. "You did a good day's work," he says after a while. He doesn't look at her. "You're a strong girl."

"Thanks." She blows her smoke away from him, but she doesn't put the cigarette out. It's nearly dark, the apartments across the parking lot are smudged, empty-looking. A car pulls into the space for Number 1, two men get out. They're arguing about something, Liv can hear by the tone of their voices, though she can't tell what the argument's about. Probably just bickering, dumb bickering, the kind she and her father do all day.

"I called Sam," he says out of nowhere.

18

By noon the next day her father has finished his work on the reef. Four dozen abs—reds and greens—are heaped in a pile, covered with wet burlap bags. Sitting on an upended milk crate, he looks tired and satisfied. He polishes off two PBJs, chewing them carefully, deliberately, washing them down with water. "Kimchi?" he says, lifting the jar like a toast.

"No, thanks."

"Gotta try new things." He shakes his head. Pulling a long, slimy strand of cabbage out of the jar, he lowers it into his upturned mouth. "What are you drawing?"

She looks up from her pastel sketch of the coastline, clouds billowing up from behind the hills. "That," she says, with a jerk of her chin. Keeps on sketching.

"See if Spinuchi's wet suit will fit you," he says, and belches.

"What?" Hearing Spinuchi's name cartwheels her heart.

"Are you hard of hearing? See if you can fit Spinuchi's wet suit."

"Why?"

"Humor me," he says.

She fills in the trunk of a tree, carefully, deliberately, with the side of her chalk. She feels him watching, his impatience with her. At last she closes her sketchbook, puts it in her backpack along with the box of pastels. She does this the way he does things, slowly and with maddening care. Only then does she rummage through the lidded box until she finds the top half of a wet suit. This one has a bright red lining. The Farmer Johns have a matching red stripe.

"Try it on." He waits, arms crossed on his black rubber chest.

She waits for him to turn around. *"Well?"*

"Well, what?"

"Turn around!" she says.

"What? Oh, yeah. Okay." He turns so that his back is to her. "Should fit," he says. "You're about the same height." The back of his neck is red. Is he actually embarrassed, or is it just the sun?

Liv shucks off her jeans. It's hard getting her legs into the Farmer Johns, but finally she wriggles them up to her waist. Her father's right, they're about her size. She slips out of her shirt and T-shirt, pulls on the jumper, and zips up the jacket with the bright red lining. It's big in the shoulders but otherwise fits. "Okay," she says. "You can turn around." She remembers for some crazy reason the night of the freshman dance, the way Suds's father looked when Suds came down the stairs in her prom dress. Liv had felt like a bridesmaid, no one to fuss over her. Except Gran, of course, always Gran.

"Huh," he says, checking her out. Then: "Wanna have a look around?"

She glances quickly at the water. "In there?"

"Yeah, in there." He smiles, just a crack.

"Are there sharks?"

"Sure, there's sharks. We probably won't see any, but, yeah, they're down there all right."

"Well, what do you do if you see one?" She's stalling, which he probably knows. He's like Mr. Denker, but only in this one way: if she can get him talking about something he loves, he'll never shut up.

"Depends," he says. "Most of them don't want anything to do with you. You ignore them. Blues, leopards . . ."

"But what if they do want to . . . eat you. Or something."

"Well, if it's a white, it might do some good to whack him on the nose, or roll yourself up into a ball so you don't look like a seal. Seal's what he wants, not you. But mostly, you just want to get your butt out of there."

"Oh," she gulps.

"Come on," he says, standing. "You can come right back to the boat if you don't like it." He searches the storage locker until he finds two masks with round glass faces and two orange-tipped black snorkels. "These will do," he says, frowning. He spits into one of the masks, two big gobs, then rinses the spit out with seawater. He grins at the look on her face. "Here, do the same with this one, so it won't fog up." She spits and rinses, pulls the mask gingerly over her head. He pulls it off, adjusting it several times until he's satisfied. Then he attaches the snorkel. "I'd have had you doing this when you were two," he says, "if you'd been living with me."

"Why wasn't I?" she says, behind her mask.

"What? Living with me?" He drops over the side and into the water. "Because you were living with your grandmother."

Liv stares speechlessly at her father, who looks up at her through the water-spotted glass of his mask. "Well, come on," he says. "We don't have all day."

Liv, her heart pounding, sits clumsily on the edge of the boat, her feet dangling in the water.

"Come on, come on," he says impatiently. Surprising herself, she drops into the water, yelping as the icy cold water seeps into the space between her body and the suit. But in seconds she's almost comfortable.

"Okay, now you need to learn how to clear that snorkel." The lesson goes on and on. First he explains, then he shows her what he means, then he explains again. She watches him, she puts her face in the water, fills the snorkel with water, blows it out. He explains some more. He makes her do it again and again. "Okay," he says at last. "Let's go." He grabs her hand and she skims along beside him, his big fins moving them like propellers on the surface of the swells. It's the first time she's ever held her father's hand. In her whole life. Right now.

They skim along the side of a forest of reddish-yellow stalks of kelp and she spots her first fish, then another, weaving through the forest, thin silvery fish that couldn't be less bothered by their passing.

At first she's disappointed that it's not like pictures she's seen of Hawaii or the Caribbean, places she'd tried to get Gran to go. This is different, not as clear, grayish-blue, filled with bits of yellow stuff like dust. The bottom, which looks far away, though it's hard to tell how far, is furry-looking, humped. There are things moving down there. Small fish rise toward them, curious.

Then the bottom drops away, fast. They are moving toward deeper, darker blue water. She grabs harder on to her father's calloused hand, twice the size of hers, which isn't small.

They have come to a kind of underwater garden, and suddenly there are fish everywhere, all sizes and colors, the soft pastel grays and blues of her chalks. They poke around red sea fans looking for food, dart in and out of caves. Her father points at something she can't at first see. Then an ugly fat snakelike face pokes out of one of the caves. Her father lets go of her hand, dives toward the cave. The snake—is it an eel?—retreats, then sneaks out again once it thinks her father is gone. Liv floats, trying to memorize all the plant life so that she can ask him later what everything is called. This is his world. When she was living in New

York, in the city, this is what her father was doing, this is part of what she never knew about him. She watches him swim around the reef, playful, graceful as a seal. She's too fascinated to think about the fact that she's no longer attached to his hand.

She is disappointed when it's time to return to the tiny world of the boat. "That was great, Dad!" she says, too filled with excitement to be cautious with her words.

"Yeah," he mumbles, "clear day for a change."

It's still early and so they cruise more slowly down the coast than they might have. "Here. Take this." Uneremoniously he turns the wheel over to Liv. "Keep her at 105," he says, tapping the compass—and goes into the cabin. Suddenly the *Jeannie T* is hers, she who doesn't even have a driver's license. She grips the wheel with both hands, not daring to change the speed or the direction a fraction of a mark off course. The wind blows her hair every which way and she knows her makeup has all washed off, but it doesn't matter. For once, she's not what she looks like.

Then suddenly, to the left of the boat in the dark streaming water, a long silver shape, then another and another, appearing and disappearing. "Dolphins!" she cries. Spinuchi's dolphins! "Dad! Dad!"

He pokes his head out of the cabin, a can of beer in his hand. "What the hell are you yelling about?"

"Dolphins!" she cries again. "Look!"

He comes up to look. "Oh, yeah," he says, like it's nothing at all.

Just ahead of the bow two dolphins leap together, two sleek silver-gray shapes in the air, curved, and at the top of their arc almost still. They re-enter the water without a splash. "Oh, man! Oh, man!" she cries. Gran's *got* to be watching this! The dolphins escort the *Jeannie T* almost as far as the harbor, crisscrossing under the bow, occasionally leaping in tandem as if for pure joy. Then they disappear into the dark water, as quickly as they came.

"Let's go over to Sam's boat," Liv says, after they've off-loaded the abs to the processor and berthed the *Jeannie T.* She can't wait to tell Sam about her day, the snorkeling, the dolphins. And besides, she knows Sam wants to see her father. She won't seek him out, though. They're both so . . . childish, so *stubborn*.

Gran used to say Liv was stubborn, and she is, sometimes. But not like her father, not like him.

"She's probably not home," he says. He fusses with everything, and then goes back and fusses some more. It takes him forever to get everything absolutely the way it's supposed to be.

"How do you know?"

"I *don't* know."

"Then why don't we go over?"

"You go ahead," he says. "I'll go up and shower."

"Well, I brought some stuff to shower, too," she says. "We can go to Sam's after."

He looks up from the box where he's refitted the contents in several ways. "Why all this stuff about Sam?"

"Dad . . . !"

"What?"

"Don't you know what you're doing?"

"Of course I know what I'm doing. I'm coiling this rope at the moment."

"You're avoiding her."

"Sam? Now, why would I be doing that?" He shakes the coils from the rope and starts all over again, making sure the loops are exactly the same size. It takes all his concentration, his brow furrowed. When she doesn't answer, he peers up, still frowning.

"Because she's sick," Liv says.

"Oh come on, Liv. What kind of a jerk do you think I am?" He laughs shortly. "Don't answer that."

"Okay then, you tell me why you've been avoiding Sam."

"You know what, kid?" He drops the lid on the locker with a bang. "It just isn't any of your business." His eyes are hard again, the pupils like daggers.

Her throat thickens and she turns. "You're right," she says. "It's none of my business. Nothing about you is my business. Never has been."

"Liv—"

But she doesn't turn around. Her clothes tucked under her arm, she wends her way through the boats, leaving him behind.

19

LIV KNOCKS ON THE ROOF of *Lady Lore*'s cabin. Sam's face appears in between the parted lace curtains. She does a classic double take at the sight of Liv ankle to neck in a black rubber wet suit.

Liv climbs in, wades through a pile of bedding to the cabin. Sam is sitting at her table removing nail polish with a cotton swab. There's an open can of root beer and a pack of gum at her right hand. "Come on in, girl!" Sam laughs, but her enthusiasm sounds forced. Liv worries for a minute that she shouldn't have just dropped in. Sam has a telephone, after all. "Tell me what in the world you've been up to. Wanna root beer?" Sam's eyes are puffy, tired-looking, and she hasn't done anything with her hair. It halos around her narrow face in an explosion of snarled curls. Her cabin is as messy as Liv's father's apartment is neat. There are magazines and record albums everywhere, unwashed dishes, tangles of clothing.

Sam slides a stick of gum from the pack and offers it to Liv. "My new addiction," she says. "Gotta quit smoking."

Liv knows it's been a workday for Sam, but she doesn't look as if she's spent the day at Shear Magic. "Did you work today?"

Sam's eyebrows go up. "Sure. Just got home." She squints down at the file going back and forth over her thumbnail. "Where's your dad?" She tries to make the question sound like just another part of the conversation, but it's more than that.

"In the shower," Liv says, not knowing how else to answer, whether or not her father will be coming over. "He took me snorkeling," she says. "Can you believe it?"

Sam looks up from the file, her eyes wide. "He did? How was it?"

"Great! It was great! I loved it." Liv tells Sam everything she can remember.

Sam files away, smiling, shaking her head. "You're one brave child," she says.

"I was scared to death!" says Liv. "But he made me feel . . . I don't know"—she shrugs—"like I could do it."

"Uptown gal takes to the ocean! Who would have thunk it!"

"Downtown girl," Liv corrects her. She leans back, slumps into herself. "It seems so far away now, New York," she says. "It's scary, kind of . . ."

"Scary?"

"Yeah, like it's all over. Forever. New York, my friends,

Gran. Well, Gran, of course. But it's all gone, you know? All of it. My whole life!"

"You can always go back, sweetie. It's just a plane ride away. But I know what you mean."

"You do?"

"Sure. I've had three, no four, very different lives. We just move on is all. Life changes, we change with it. People say that's what it means to grow. Could be true, I guess. But change can bring a lot of heartache with it, I know that."

"What other lives?"

"Oh Lord, now I've gone and done it, haven't I? Well, when we've got a lot of time and nothing better to do, I'll tell you, don't worry. We'll start with the cowgirl life. In Wyoming."

"Cool! When was that?"

"Here, give me your hand. We'll do your nails."

Liv, still caught up in the idea of other lives, lets Sam take her right hand. "So . . . when?"

"Well, Wyoming was after my hippie life and before my skydiving years."

"You jumped out of an airplane?"

"Nah." Sam laughs, cracks her gum several times. "I'm teasing you. Well, just once. I jumped once. It wasn't exactly a life."

"How come you never got married?"

Sam swivels the file expertly over Liv's rough fingernails. "Oh, I almost got married. Several times. Escaped by the hair of my chinny-chin-chin!"

"So, Dad's right?" For some reason Liv is surprised. "You don't want to be married?"

Sam looks up, eyebrows lifted. "He said that?"

"Yeah."

"Did he tell you I asked him?"

"To marry you? You *did*?"

"Yup. Figured he wasn't going to do it."

"What did he say?"

"Well, he didn't say yes. Didn't say no, come to think of it. He just"—she opens a bottle of clear nail polish—"changed the subject." She chuckles, remembering. "He's a piece of work, your father."

"You're telling me!"

After Sam has polished Liv's fingernails, which now look almost good, Liv takes Sam's key card, soap, shampoo, and a towel up to the women's bathroom. In the shower she takes her time, letting the hot water soak into her chilled body. She can still feel inside herself what it was like to move over the water. Almost more unbelievable than the fact that she snorkeled in the deep water of the Pacific is that, for the first time in her life, she was holding her father's hand.

To her disappointment her father is not on Sam's boat when she returns to it. Sam is straightening up, folding her down comforter, stacking pillows. Liv dries her hair, rubbing it hard with the towel.

"Liv?"

Liv comes out of the towel. "Huh? I mean, what did you say?"

"Did you notice your hair is kind of . . . growing out?"

"Yeah," says Liv. "Could you dye it for me?"

"Sure. I *could*. You want to keep the orange?"

"Tangerine," Liv corrects her. "Yeah, why?"

"Oh, I don't know." Sam pulls her own hair back, clipping it with a tortoiseshell barrette. "I thought maybe we could give you a trim. Get to the natural stuff. See how it looks. Then you can decide."

Liv gives Sam a suspicious look. "I know you don't like the tips."

"Honestly? No." She smiles. "But that doesn't mean you shouldn't have them. It's *your* hair." She rummages through the plastic box and comes up with a pair of scissors. She clicks them open and closed several times, her green eyes challenging. "How about it?"

"Okay," Liv agrees. "Only you'll do it back the way I want if I don't like it, right? Promise?"

"Absolutely. Come on, we'll sit outside. Then we won't get hair all over." She passes Liv a wicker bench to sit on.

It takes Sam less than ten minutes. All the time she's cutting she says, "Very nice. Yup. Pretty color, lots of red highlights. Just a little more off the back. Oh, Liv, you're gonna love it!" Finally, she hands Liv a hand mirror.

Liv looks at her face, no longer pale. Her cheeks are pink, and the rest of her face has gotten some of Sam's dreaded sun. She checks out her hair. It's chestnut brown now and feathers softly around her face. "What do you call this?" she asks Sam, frowning at her new image.

"*Pretty*, sweetheart. I call that pretty."

A sudden breeze lifts Liv's cut hair from the deck, sends it in shreds of black and orange sailing out into the water of the harbor.

As Liv hands Sam the mirror, she spots her father. "Here comes Dad," she says.

"Wait till he sees you!" Sam says delightedly.

He's halfway down the ramp, a red-and-white chicken bucket under his arm, when he stops. Now he's walking slowly toward them, a puzzled frown on his face, as if he's suddenly lost his way. He stops ten feet from the boat, his dark eyes wider than Liv's ever seen them.

"What's the matter?" she says.

His mouth is slightly ajar, his face drained of its usual color. He's staring at her with an intensity that makes her squirm. "I brought you this chicken," he says at last, handing the bucket over to Sam, his eyes still on Liv. "I can't stick around. I—" Without another word he turns on his heel and strides away.

"Mark?" Sam cradles the bucket of chicken, watching Liv's father heading up the ramp, a baffled look on her face. "What's his problem now?" Then she turns to Liv again. "Uh-oh."

"What?"

She bites the inside of her lip, considering. "Did your mother have short hair?"

"Yes." Her mother in the faded black-and-white snapshot, her shy smile. She is wearing a white sundress, the ruffled sundress of a child. Her hair is dark, darker than Liv's, and as short as Liv's is now.

"He just saw your mother," says Sam. "In you. That's why he spooked."

Liv stands, impatiently brushes hair from her shirt. "I'm hungry. Let's eat." But the look on his face stays with her. "You can dye it back tomorrow, right?" She climbs into the boat, Sam behind her.

Halfway into the boat Sam stops. "The biopsy's tomorrow, Liv," she says quietly. "That's why I took off the polish. You're not supposed to wear any. Why, I don't know . . ."

Liv's heart does a back flip. "It's *Thursday*, you said it was Thursday!"

Sam takes the bucket into the cabin and sets it on the table. "It was. They called this morning and rescheduled. The surgeon's got a golf game on Thursday. Or something." She tries to get a laugh out of Liv, who can't quite get her breath.

"It was supposed to be Thursday." A choking cry escapes her. She slumps into the bench seat. The red-and-white chicken bucket looks too festive. Like only happy people are supposed to eat it.

Sam's hand cups Liv's shoulder. "Hey! It's okay. Better to get it over with, right? The sooner—"

"We've got to tell Dad!" Liv gets half up, then collapses back into her seat.

"I'll tell him, sweetie. Don't worry."

Liv's afraid to ask, afraid she knows the answer, but she asks anyway: "Do you want me to go with you?"

Sam's green eyes search Liv's. Between them, the stupid red-and-white bucket. "Do you want to?"

She doesn't, but she knows she should. Slowly, she nods.

"Well, okay then. If you're sure. It's at nine o'clock," Sam says. "And it's probably going to take a while. Better bring a book or something." She hesitates for a moment, biting her lip. "Thanks, Liv. I didn't know that I'd need somebody out there waiting for me until right this minute."

"Are you scared?"

"Moi?" Her joking façade crumbles. "Hell, yes, I'm scared."

"But it's going to be all right, isn't it?"

"Yeah, it's going to be fine." She knocks on the teak behind her head. "For luck," she says. "Now let's eat. I can't have anything but water after eight, but nobody said I couldn't eat half a bucket of chicken before then!"

But all she does is nibble on a wing, looking far away, intent on her own thoughts. Liv, with her sea-hunger, eats like a starving predator. She's got to tell her father about tomorrow. Call him somehow without Sam's catching on. Liv doesn't know exactly why she wants to give the Tin Man another chance. He doesn't deserve one. But Sam needs all the support she can get.

Liv thinks about how it must have been for Gran that last day. She's thought about it often, tried to picture the scene in her mind—maybe because she couldn't be there, couldn't help—Gran being carried out of her kitchen—they found her in the kitchen, Liv knows that much—by strangers, in the hands of strangers. Gran would have tried to hold on. She would have tried her hardest to hold on until Liv came, Liv knows that. She shudders, rubs her arms.

"Cold?"

"Huh? Oh yeah. A little. From diving, I guess. Can I have your card again?"

Sam pushes the card across the table.

"Sure is a long way to go for a pee!"

Liv goes straight to the pay phone outside the restrooms, drops a coin in. "Be there, Dad," she says. The phone rings four times. Liv wraps the cord around and around her thumb. He answers on the sixth ring.

"Dad? Liv."

"Huh?"

"It's Liv. *Olivia*, your daughter."

"I know who it is."

"Sam's operation is tomorrow, Dad. They changed it to tomorrow morning."

Silence. Then: "Huh."

"I just thought you should know."

She hears him moving something around. The skillet? Shells? He mutters some words away from the phone that sound like a curse. Then: "Do you want me to pick you up?"

"I think I'll stay here. With Sam," she says. "I'm going with her to the hospital tomorrow."

"Huh," he says. "Well."

"Deep subject, Dad," she says.

"Yeah." Weary sigh.

"*Well*, okay then. I'll see ya."

"Right," he says, and hangs up.

She stares at the receiver in her hand for a minute before dropping it into its cradle. Her father is the world's weirdest man.

Sam gives Liv a granny gown to sleep in. They laugh at the way it fits, as if she's Alice in Wonderland grown immense while her clothes stayed the same size. Exhausted, Liv drops off the minute her head hits the pillow, but she swims her way through the night, waking herself up several times to make sure she's on dry land. Each time she sees that Sam is still awake, reading a book, a flashlight clutched under her chin.

20

"SAM? OLIVIA?"

It's dark. Liv doesn't remember where she is. She's sure she heard her name, but where the voice is coming from isn't clear at first. She's been deep in sleep, deep into dreaming, but the voice has chased the dream into hiding. Then Sam's voice: "Mark?"

Has he come to take Liv diving?

The canvas parts and there's the dark figure of her father leaning in. "Aren't you up yet? I thought you were going to the hospital." He folds back the canvas to the gray morning light.

"What little bird told you that?" Sam yawns, stretches, and groans. "Did you bring us some coffee?"

"Nope," he says with a satisfied smirk. "Olivia's in charge of coffee now. Give her a hundred bucks and she will buy you one nice little coffeepot." He climbs in, chuckling to himself, and begins to roll the canvas back. It's an overcast morning, the half-ring of mountains cupping the harbor blue-gray with wisps of cloud. All around the *Lady Lore*, caught in a dance with the onshore breeze, masts sing their discordant songs.

Liv asks her father, just to tease, if he's brought her toothbrush. To her complete surprise, he whips it out of his back pocket.

"Unreal," she says.

"What? This is yours, isn't it?"

"Yes." She grins. "It's mine."

"Well, I'll leave you two to get ready. What's our ETD?"

"ETD?" Liv giggles.

"Estimated Time of Departure, sailor," Sam drawls. "Eight-thirty," she tells Liv's father. "Are you sure you want to take the day off? It's going to be a while, you know."

"I'm here, aren't I?"

Sam looks at Liv, her mouth pursed to keep from laughing, her eyebrows drawn together. "He's here, isn't he?" mimicking his deep voice.

"Yup," Liv laughs. "He's here."

"Okay then," he says, missing—maybe ignoring—the joke. "I'll be back at eight-twenty." And he's gone.

"You're going to be sorry," Sam warns Liv. "You're the one who's got to wait with him. When he doesn't have something to do with his hands, some engine part, he goes nuts. He'll be climbing the walls by the time I'm out of surgery."

Surgery. The word sends chills down Liv's back. "Don't worry," she says, folding up her bedding. "I can handle Dad."

Sam is standing on her comforter, a pillow under her arm, studying Liv. There's an unreadable look on her face. "Huh," she says softly, in a perfect imitation of Liv's father.

The hospital is smaller than Mercy, not as intimidating. Massive arms of oak trees hang protectively over the entrance. Inside, flowers and plants, nice furniture and paintings, like a rich person's living room. Liv is nervous just the same, though she is determined not to show it.

This is *different*, she assures herself. This isn't Gran, this is *different*. Still, it feels too much the same.

Her father herds them through the corridors, as if he knows just where to go, and sure enough, there's the sign for Surgery.

Liv expects to wait around for a while, which is always what happens with doctors, but almost immediately Sam is drawn away by a nurse with a clipboard.

"Wait!" booms Liv's father. "Where are you going?"

His voice is so loud, both Sam and the nurse turn, wide-eyed. Neither answer. Everyone looks up, the clerks at the desk, a passing doctor, a child with frightened blue eyes. For a minute, everything stops, her father in the middle looking foolish, lost.

Liv pulls on his arm. "Come on, Dad. We've got to wait in the waiting room."

He turns, seems surprised to see her on his arm. "What?" Looks back at Sam. "Where are they taking you? How will we know where to find you?" People look away now, as if they're embarrassed for him.

"Don't worry," the nurse says, "we'll find you in the waiting room and take you to her."

"When?" he demands. "How long will it be? Will it be long?"

"Dad," Liv coaxes, "come on. It's all right."

Sam blows them a kiss and winks. She follows the nurse down a long corridor.

"Damn," he says, "I didn't think . . . I didn't think they'd, just, just . . ." He runs a hand back over his thinning hair.

"Did you have your coffee?" Liv asks. Until this minute she thought she'd be the one to break down, but her father has taken care of all that. "We can go to the cafeteria. Sam said it would be a while." He follows her like a sleepwalker.

The fluorescent lights inside the cafeteria are harsh and bright, there are open pipes in the ceiling and long tube-like things going in all directions. People's voices have a hollow sound, their laughter echoing as if they're all in a cave. Liv picks up a tray, a plastic spoon; her father follows her as she gathers a carton of yogurt, a stale-looking dough-nut, an apple for later. He pours himself a cup of coffee, frowning.

"How much do you know about all this?" he says when they're sitting across from each other at a table with a scratched Formica top and coffee rings. The cafeteria is nearly full. There are people like the two of them, obviously visiting, while others dressed in green uniforms or flowered smocks laugh and chatter. It surprises Liv, still, that life can just go on.

"About the operation?"

"Well, yeah. About what she has. You know . . ." He dumps three packets of sugar into his coffee, stirring it vigorously, frowning all the while.

And so she explains what she knows. Sam is having a biopsy, she says. He knows *that*, he says, but he doesn't seem to know anything at all about what can happen if it's cancer. She explains about lumpectomies and mastectomies as best she can, feeling sick inside. She doesn't want to think about all this. Sam isn't sick. She's just here for a test. But her father knows nothing, and so she has to explain.

He listens intently, his eyes piercing hers. "Why didn't she tell me all this stuff?"

"You weren't around, Dad. She tried."

"Hmmph," he says, leaning back in his chair. "She didn't try very hard."

They return to the waiting room. Liv picks up a tattered copy of *National Geographic* and sticks on her Walkman. Anything to stop thinking about the last time, about waiting to hear about her Gran, about Rosa the nurse and the way her eyes said everything before her words did. Liv hadn't been ready. Maybe she *should* think about Sam, expect all the terrible things that her mind doesn't want to face. Then she won't be shocked out of her skin if something bad happens.

Gran always said, "Expect the best, but prepare for the worst." How could you do both? Gran's sayings got so monotonous after a while that Liv had stopped listening, stopped wondering what they meant. But now she thinks they might have been road signs to places she herself has not yet been. Now she has to find her way without them.

Her father sits with his arms crossed, his long legs stuck out in front of him. There are holes in the knees of his jeans. Holes are all right with him, she's learned that. Dirt is not okay, holes are okay. Nine-thirty-five says the round school clock on the wall. He gets up, riffles through a stack of shredded magazines, flips open a copy of *Sports Illustrated*. Sam is right, Liv's father can't keep still. He's up and down every couple of minutes.

She feels a tap on her shoulder. Startled, she looks up, pulls away an earpiece.

"How can a person talk to you when you've got that . . . that *thing* on your head!"

"Oh." She lifts off her Walkman, puts it carefully into her backpack. "I guess a person can't." She's learning that it's more fun to go along with him than to fight him. He doesn't know what to do with her if she doesn't fight back.

He stares at her. "Well," he says at last, "I guess they can't."

"What did you want to talk about?" She crosses her arms and gets comfortable, as if she's ready for a nice long chat.

"Me? I don't know. Nothing." He gets up, walks over to the water cooler, takes a sip. "Mercury," he says.

"What?"

"There's mercury in water fountains. Shouldn't drink out of them."

It's ten o'clock, then ten-fifteen. The minutes crawl. "You need anything from the gift shop?" he says. "They probably have flowers, right?"

"Oh, yeah! Good idea. Get anything but white. White's for, well, for funerals and stuff. Oh, and pink. You probably don't want to get pink. That's for new moms."

"Huh. Well, what's left?"

"Red," Liv says. "Red is for love. Didn't you know that? Want me to come with you?"

"No, no. Stay here. In case they come looking for us. I'll be back in a couple of minutes. If they tell you what room she's in, write it down so you won't forget!" He strides away, straight-backed and purposeful now that he has a mission.

He returns, carrying a spring bouquet in an ugly green vase. "How about this? It's all colors. Can't go wrong with something like this, right?" He looks very pleased with himself. "They didn't have any roses."

"It's pretty, Dad. She'll like it."

"You think so?"

"I'm sure," she says.

"I was thinking . . ." He sits down, the vase stuck between his knees. "She might not get to come home. I mean, if it's . . . bad."

"Don't say that!" she cries.

"Gotta face things, Liv," he says seriously. "Head on. Gotta face things head on. No point in ducking the hard stuff. It just comes back and bites you on the butt."

Is he serious? "Face things? Is that what you do?"

"Of course that's what I do. You can't go around with your head stuck up your . . . stuck in the sand!"

She shakes her head, speechless.

"What?"

"Nothing." Where could she begin with him? With her birth? Just how long did he stick around that time? Would he even listen?

"So you don't think it's going to be bad, huh? With Sam?" He loves Sam, it's in his eyes. Liv sees it clearly, for the first time.

"It isn't," she insists, for both of them.

"Mr. Trager?"

He's out of the chair in a shot. "Yes?"

"You and your daughter can come back now. Your . . . friend is in recovery."

Liv follows her father, her father follows the nurse, pelting her back with questions. "Well, what's she got? Is she all right, or what? Is she awake? Can she go home?"

"The doctor will answer all your questions," says the nurse. She steps into one of the rooms, her father follows. Liv stops outside the door, can't go inside. But she can't keep herself from peering in.

In the stark white bed Sam's asleep, her face pale as . . . pale as death. A wave of dizziness washes over Liv. She steadies herself against the door frame until her head clears.

"Samantha?" says the nurse, leaning over Sam. "You can wake up now."

They all wait for Sam to follow orders, Liv's father by the

side of the bed, Liv outside the door holding her breath. They wait for Sam to flutter open her eyes and smile wanly but bravely, like in the movies. She doesn't. The nurse lifts Sam's wrist, feels for a pulse, frowns at her watch, sets the wrist down.

"Well, what's going on?"

Liv realizes that her father probably doesn't know how to whisper. He's used to yelling over the growl of boat engines. If he's not yelling, he's probably not talking.

"Is she all right?" His voice booming.

Liv wants to get out of there, make all this go away before it gets worse. Her heart thumps painfully, as if it knows something terrible, something her mind won't accept.

"She'll wake up in a minute," the nurse says.

A woman with long honey-blond hair and a white smock strides past Liv into the room. Around her neck hangs the snake of a stethoscope. "Mr. Trager?" she says, offering a small pointed hand for him to shake.

"Nice to meet you," he says, pumping her hand. "Can you get Sam's doctor for me? Her doctor is supposed to come and tell us what's going on."

"I am her doctor," with weary patience, as if she has to say this all the time. "Dr. Kaufman."

He has enough good grace to look a little sheepish. "Oh," he says. Then he's back to his regular self. "Well? How is Sam, then? Does she, you know—"

"Have a malignancy? We won't be able to tell that until they run the . . ."

"Hey, you guys."

Liv's father and the doctor turn. "Ah," says Dr. Kaufman, "she's awake now." Liv takes a cautious step inside the door.

Sam reaches out a hand to Liv's father. He holds out the vase of flowers, then realizes she wants his hand and passes the flowers to the doctor, who doesn't seem to know what to do with them either. A look passes between Liv's father and Sam that excludes everybody in the room, her too. But Liv doesn't mind. Just hearing Sam's voice makes everything all right again.

"This has been very hard on us," Liv's father says to Sam. It's his best joke so far. Sam rewards him with a tired smile. "Does she get to go home now?" he asks Dr. Kaufman.

"Sure does. As soon as she feels ready."

"Well, okay. Good. You got a wheelchair around here?"

The doctor looks puzzled. "What for?"

"You don't expect her to walk out of here, do you? She's just had surgery!" He's still holding her hand. It's clear to Liv that her father's doing the holding on, and not the other way around.

21

BY MID-AUGUST, it's hot as New York, but dry, dry and windy.

"Santa Anas," her father says, as they head into the harbor, Liv's hair, longer now, blowing around her head. "Devil winds."

At the loading dock Liv is hooking the bag of abalones to the winch when she hears her father say, "You still got that cast on, kid?"

Liv looks up, and there's Spinuchi with his cast and his wide, happy grin. "Two more days," he says, "then I'll be ready for work."

"You'll be ready for school is what you'll be," Liv's father mutters. "You, too," he says, with a jerk of his chin toward Liv.

School. Liv doesn't want to think about it.

"Want to make yourself useful? You can do some errands for me tomorrow. Show Liv where Rod's Marine is, maybe get some groceries while you're at it."

"Sure!" Spinuchi says happily. "I mean, if it's okay with you, Liv."

Liv shrugs. "Sure." Won't look at him, though. She's been thinking about Brian Spinuchi, more than she wants to. He's got to have a girlfriend. How could a guy who looks like Spinuchi not be going with somebody?

On the phone, later, with Suds: "You remember . . . The guy I told you about. I said you'd be in love, like, immediately! You don't remember? Oh. Well, we're going out tomorrow. Well, not like a date or anything . . . No, it's not a date. Well, sure he likes me . . ." Suds starts telling her something about Paula, a new friend. Now it's Suds and Megan and Paula. Well, it's not as if she expected them to save her place. But still . . .

"Ready?" Spinuchi in the doorway, white T-shirt, faded jeans riding his hipbones. His cast, covered with autographs and crude drawings, hangs from his neck in a bright blue sling, the color of his eyes.

"You sure you can drive?" Liv's father comes up behind Liv and pokes his head out at Spinuchi, who's been driving his mom's car every day since the accident.

"I'm getting pretty good with my left hand," Spinuchi says.

Liv's father gives him the kind of look that passes only between men. Then he reaches into his pocket and hands Spinuchi the truck keys. "Be careful," he says, "that's my work truck."

Liv's father has given her a list of things she's never heard of. She has money for groceries, too, but no list for that.

"I like your hair," Spinuchi says, as they cross the lot to the pickup. "It's . . . I don't know. Different!"

"Oh, yeah, like you can't tell it's not the same color!" She laughs, so he does, too. "I'm thinking of going blond, blond with maybe some . . . chartreuse. No, *purple!*" she teases. "Only kidding."

"You look like a completely different person, I mean, with your new clothes and everything."

"My new *old* clothes. Yeah. I'm just like everybody else now."

He stops, his left hand on the truck door. "You're not like anybody else, Liv. Not like anybody I know . . ."

"Is that good? Is that good, Brian Spinuchi?" She gives him her straight-brow most serious look.

"Yup," he says happily, "that's good."

They both get into the truck.

"Uh-oh," says Spinuchi, when they've slammed the heavy doors of the old Chevy pickup. "I forgot one thing."

"What's that?"

"My mom's car's an automatic." He thinks for a minute. "Can you shift?"

She doesn't know how, never tried. "It can't be that hard. Can you believe Dad didn't think about this?"

"I guess he's not perfect." Spinuchi laughs.

"Oh, he's not perfect," Liv drawls. "Believe me."

Spinuchi shows Liv how to move the gearshift from low to second to high. "You gotta sit over here, Liv," he says. "Don't worry, I don't bite. Not Mark Trager's daughter, I don't!"

She doesn't know if she's happy about that or not. But he's not her type, so she doesn't worry about it for long.

Just what her type is, she's forgotten. Guys with punk hair and John Lennon glasses? It amuses her that she wouldn't be recognized in the city now, in her old neighborhood or at school. She could pass like a raggedy ghost through the halls. Suds and Megan would try to hide her until she came to her senses. She giggles, thinking about how much fun it would be to show up in her latest incarnation, thrift-store jeans and baggy men's shirts, watermelon lip gloss, no color at all.

There could be something seriously wrong with a person who changes like a chameleon, couldn't there?

Maybe not. Gran would call it "trying on lives." Gran would like this latest Liv.

"Okay," says Spinuchi, when she's gone through the gears several times, "you ready?"

"Yup."

They buck across the parking lot and stall the engine. Liv whips around to check the door to Number 5, but her father hasn't come running out. They try again. This time, with just a little gear grinding, they get it. She's close enough to Spinuchi to smell him, which is close. He smells like soap, as if he just came from the shower. "Okay, shift!"

he says, and she shifts into high gear. They cruise along, proud of themselves.

"It's funny that you never tried to drive a car before," Spinuchi says. "I was driving my dad's car up and down the driveway when I was thirteen."

"Oh, cars aren't such a big thing in the city," she says. "We didn't even own one, Gran and me."

"How did you, like, go out on dates and stuff?"

"Horses," Liv says.

He grins, so ready to believe anything she says.

"Nah, subways."

"Oh, yeah . . ." he says uncertainly.

"I guess I'll have to get a car, huh?"

But he doesn't answer that. "Do you think your dad would let you go out with me?" he says as she shifts into third. "I mean, if you want to." She can feel him looking at her. She keeps her eyes on the road, as if she's really doing the driving.

They come to a stop at the one traffic light. It changes to green. "Okay, shift into first," he says.

Liv pretends that the shifting takes every bit of her concentration, that way she doesn't have to look at him. But she has to say something. "You know, it's funny. I don't know if I'm supposed to ask my father about going out, or what . . ."

"Well, I'm gonna take a wild guess and say that he's going to expect you to ask him. Are you kidding? Mark Trager? He'd probably come along as a bodyguard!"

Liv remembers joking with Gran about having to get a bodyguard. It was their last talk, one of the last things Gran said.

"Okay, now second," Spinuchi says, and as she pushes up the gearshift, he ducks his head and gives her a quick kiss on the lips. Then he throws his head back and howls like a coyote. "I just kissed Mark Trager's daughter!"

"Sort of," she says, her heart thumping, her lips still tingling.

"Yeah," he laughs, "sort of. Wasn't much of a kiss, huh? For a city girl, I mean. Maybe I can try again sometime."

She hopes her cheeks aren't as red as she thinks they might be. "Maybe. Sometime. Only do me a favor and warn me first."

He gives her one of his rare serious looks. "Okay, Liv Trager."

"Olivia to you," she says.

"Olivia?"

"I'm kidding, I'm kidding. Liv is fine."

They stop in several places, serious and purposeful now because there's this careful thing happening between them. Spinuchi looks at her more often with a kind of expectation that both excites and terrifies her; she notices things about him, nice things she hadn't noticed before. Like the fact that he has clean fingernails, clean rounded-off nails that look as strong as horse's hooves. But he walks slightly pigeon-toed, and he hooks his thumbs in his pockets, as if he doesn't know what to do with his hands either. He's not exactly perfect, which is good.

There's this difference now in how they are, and Liv doesn't know what to make of it, or if it's even good. All because of a kiss. One silly little kiss has changed everything.

The last stop is the grocery store. On the way in, Spinuchi asks how Sam is doing. "I was going to ask you before," he says apologetically. "I guess there were other things on my mind."

"Oh?" she teases. "Like what?"

He grins. He clears his throat. He sticks his hands in his back pockets. "I don't know . . . stuff."

"Sam's fine," Liv says.

"That's great!" Spinuchi grabs a shopping cart, pulls it from the stack. "I'll bet you're relieved, huh?"

She looks at him for a moment, her mind having gone back to the hospital room, back to the truth, which is that she doesn't really know that Sam is fine. Nobody knows that yet. "Oh. Oh, yeah."

"Pickles and liverwurst," Spinuchi says, while she's picking out bread, thinking how strange it is not to know if your own father likes wheat or white.

"Pickles and *what*?"

"Your dad likes liverwurst sandwiches. With pickles on them. It's probably his favorite thing."

"I can't stand the *smell* of liverwurst!" she says. "What's his second favorite?"

"I don't know. Except that he hates tuna fish."

"He does?" On the boat, her father wolfing down two of her tuna sandwiches without saying a word.

On the way home, they pass the community college set high on a hill above the harbor. Just up the coast is the university. Liv remembers that Megan's father, a biologist, once went to a conference there. He said it was one of the best schools in the country for marine biology, which is what Megan plans to major in. Megan's a brain.

"What are you going to do after graduation, Spinuchi? Are you going to be an abalone diver?" Liv's been thinking about school, wishing she were through with it so that she could just go on to college, major in something fun. But she doesn't know what that might be.

"Yeah, I guess," he says. "Or get on with the Harbor Patrol. They let me volunteer after school now, and in the summers. I'm always hanging around the office, trying to make myself useful."

"Don't you want to go to college?"

"Nah," he says, "not me. I'd never make it. Carrie—that's my sis—got all the brains in the family. And Tony, my brother. There wasn't enough to go all the way around, I guess." He grins happily, as if it's perfectly all right to be missing a brain. "How about you?"

"No idea," says Liv, but the ocean that runs like a long blue ribbon past the window seems to draw her to it. Now that she's been out there, she sees it differently. "Marine biology, maybe. I could become the world's foremost expert on abalone." She laughs.

"That wouldn't take long," Spinuchi says. "Not much to abalones."

"Don't count on it," she says. "I have a friend whose father spends his whole entire life studying the mating cycle of fruit flies."

"Whatever turns you on!" Spinuchi laughs. "Yeah, marine biology would be fun."

"Well, I have to go to college. If I don't, all Gran's money goes to a private school I hate."

"Hey, you wanna feed the ducks?" Spinuchi slows the truck, makes a left-hand turn onto a dirt drive that encircles a small lake.

"Absolutely," Liv says, biting her lip to keep from laughing. Ducks? "I love to feed ducks."

"Cool," he says. He pulls into a small parking lot at the edge of a lake. Or a pond, maybe it's a pond. There are reeds sticking up along the sides and an island of trees and bushes in the middle. "You gotta watch out for the geese, though. They bite." He digs through the grocery bags and pulls out the loaf of the white bread that Liv finally chose. Liv opens the door to get out. Already the ducks are waddling over. Fat little black birds, too. "Coots," Spinuchi says. "Here." He hands her the bread in its cellophane wrapper. "You have to tear it up into little pieces." He laughs. "Well, you don't have to. That's just what my mom used to tell me, because I'd just throw the whole slice and run!"

Liv opens the bag, tears a piece of the bread into bits, and scatters it. The ducks and birds make a beeline for it, and it's gone in three seconds.

They sit on a park bench, Liv tearing the bread so that Spinuchi can toss it left-handed.

She passes him the last of the bread. "Well, there goes Dad's liverwurst-and-pickle sandwiches. Where are the killer geese?"

"You don't believe me, huh?"

"Sure I do."

"They almost bit off my big toe when I was two years old," he says in a troubled voice, as if it happened just yesterday.

"Really?"

"They're mean!" he says. "I'm not kidding!"

Now that the bread is gone, the ducks have lost interest. Having run out of things to do, Liv and Spinuchi watch the birds peck along the edge of the pond as if they're in a movie. There's that . . . something . . . happening again, she can feel it in the space between them. It isn't just her, that's for sure.

Spinuchi lays his hand on the bench between them, his palm up. She lays her palm down flat on his. His hand is warm. He curls his fingers around hers. She looks up to see his blue eyes waiting. He tilts his face toward hers, stops halfway. "Okay?" he says.

"Yeah," she says softly, and lifts her face to meet his.

It's a perfect kiss, as if they've done it lots of times before and know just how to move their mouths. How could that be? They hardly know each other. But it's perfect just the same. They separate, breathing fast. His face is flushed; hers must be, too. He tries to get his arms around her, but the cast gets in the way. "Damn," he mutters. She giggles. He gets the cast halfway around; her arms reach up under his to touch his warm back. They're kissing again when a car pulls up behind. They break off. Kids tumble out of the car, screaming and yelling, running straight for the ducks and scattering them in all directions.

Spinuchi sighs, relaxes his arms around her. He has incredible eyes, intense one minute, sparkling with humor the next. And she loves that he's, well, sort of . . . innocent. Compared to city guys, anyway.

"Yeah," she sighs, "I know. Where are the killer geese when you need them?"

22

SAM TAKES LIV SHOPPING for school clothes. In a real store. Liv pokes through the racks, not knowing what to choose. What do kids wear to school here? Sam isn't much help. "You know what?" she says, with a thoughtful frown, "most of the kids I see look like they just came out of the thrift store. I don't know . . ."

Hours later, Liv ends up with a new pair of jeans and a plain black long-sleeved V-necked T-shirt. She puts off the shoe decision until last. Sam laughs when Liv says it's the shoes that are the most important. She knows how she'll be looked over on the first day of school, picked apart. She used to do it herself to the new girls. In seconds, she and Suds and Megan would decide where the new girl belonged, what group she belonged to, just by checking out her shoes. Never gave her a chance. Now she feels bad about it.

Sam is quieter than usual. Her mind seems to be somewhere else, or maybe she's just bored. Sam isn't a shopper. At home she collapses onto the couch while Liv boils water for tea.

"I guess you're looking forward to school, huh?" Sam says. She drops off her shoes and tucks her bare feet up under her. "Tending for your dad has been hard work."

Liv doesn't answer at first. Tending's not so hard. And she's grown to love the long days at sea. At first they had seemed uneventful, now she's aware of shifts in the wind and the currents, cloud patterns, more kinds of birds than she can name. Her body feels purposeful and strong. The idea of sitting in a classroom seems so, well, childish now. But she knows what Gran would have to say about that. "I'm not exactly looking forward to it," she says at last.

"Well, at least you've got a friend."

Liv hears her father's truck. The door slams and Liv hears Spinuchi's voice as well as her father's. They come in together. Spinuchi shoots Liv a shy, knowing smile, then glances quickly at her father to see if he's watching.

But her father, as usual, has diving on his mind. "The kid, here, is getting his cast off finally. Said I'd take him out on Saturday."

Sam glances quickly at Liv. Liv frowns to keep Sam from saying what she knows Sam is about to say. Will they be taking Liv along, or is her job over now? And if it's over, why doesn't her father say so?

Her father clamps a big hand on Spinuchi's left arm so hard he winces. "From now on, it's just weekends, though.

I'm not going to be responsible for you not graduating from high school."

Her father doesn't even look at her. Neither does Spinuchi. It's as if she never tended at all.

She and Sam make dinner while her father and Spinuchi watch TV. Like a couple of old buddies. Sam rolls her eyes. "Men," she says. "Tell them dinner's ready, will you?"

"It'll sure be nice to eat with both hands!" Spinuchi says when they've all sat down. He smears mayonnaise left-handed onto his burger bun. Liv doesn't offer to help.

The talk goes on around Liv like a stream around a rock. Dive talk, always it's dive talk. Sam looks across the table with a look of fond concern, the way Gran would if she were there. Liv tries not to feel sorry for herself, but it's hard. Tending for her father, swimming at his side, she was as close to him as she will probably ever get. But that doesn't seem to matter to him. To him, it's all just work. A tender is a tender.

While her father explains, step by step, just what he had to do to fix the neighbor's stopped-up sink—*"and this wad of hair the size of a golf ball!"*—Liv makes chocolate sundaes with the works: nuts, whipped cream, maraschino cherries, the chocolate syrup drizzled over the top. Works of art.

Not that they'll notice.

But she's wrong. "What's this?" her father demands.

"Yum!" says Sam. "I haven't had a chocolate sundae in years!"

"All this sugar isn't good for you," her father says, digging his spoon through the chocolate. He eats the whole thing, frowning.

"I, uh, need to say something." Sam clears her throat as if she's about to make a speech. Just smears of chocolate left in the four dishes, the sun nearly gone, a warm breeze through the open window. Sam looks annoyed, then almost angry, and for a crazy minute Liv thinks she's about to break up with her dad. In front of everybody.

But it isn't that.

"I got the results. It's not . . . good," she says. Golden sunlight caught in her curls, her green eyes gleaming.

Spinuchi is the first to speak. "Uh, maybe I should . . ." He scrapes back his chair, but Sam lays a hand on his wrist.

"It's okay, honey," she says, "you're practically family."

"Well, what is it?" Liv's father demands. "What did they say?"

"It's positive," she says quietly. Her mascara's smeared, giving her the traces of a black eye.

Liv's father, agitated, drums the table with his fingers. "I thought you said it wasn't good . . . !"

Sam almost smiles, then her eyes darken. "Well, positive means . . . means positive for cancer."

Liv gets up without realizing what she's doing, knocking the chair out from under her. She picks it up, places it carefully under the table. "I . . . uh . . . I gotta . . ." She turns and strides for the door.

"Where are you going?" her father bellows. "Come back here!"

"It's all right," Liv hears Sam say as she bolts through the door. "It's all right, Mark. Let her go."

Liv takes off across the gravel, already running, out into the road toward the beach, her feet thumping the concrete, passing all the shops that have now become familiar, as if, in spite of herself, this place has become home. She can't run the way she used to, but she keeps going anyway, her breath coming ragged, tears streaming off her face and into the wind she makes with her running.

So stupid to think things could be all right, that Sam was going to be fine. Stupid to believe, to let down your guard. This is what happened when you did that, you got caught like a rabbit in the lettuce. *Stupid!* Sam didn't just find out. She *knew*. She's probably known for weeks.

God, don't let her die. Don't make me go through that again.

Wiping her nose, her face, with her sleeve. What was she doing out here, anyway? This wouldn't be happening if she'd gone back to live in the city. With Suds, whatever . . . Her old running shoes hitting the sidewalk, pounding the broken sidewalk.

She stops at the lifeguard stand, bends over, clutching the cold metal rail, breathing hard. She won't stay here. Stupid to care about Sam. Who's Sam, anyway? Not her mother.

She climbs up onto the platform, leans against the wooden siding, still warm from the sun setting now in a blaze, melting on the horizon like orange sherbet.

She will never like it here, she will *not*. It fools you with its beauty.

At the edge of the water a dog with long, skinny legs— a greyhound?—lopes along. An old man and woman pass, slowly, walking arm in arm. The gulls are in a single long line, watching the sun go down. Why do they do that? What does she care? What does she care about any of this? She lays her head on her knees, wraps her arms around her tired legs.

"Liv?" She lifts her head, surprised. Spinuchi looking up at her from the bottom of the steps.

She puts her forehead back on her arms. Hears him coming up the metal steps.

He hunkers down beside her. "You okay?"

She nods.

"Your dad told me where to find you."

She laughs, a bitter sound muffled in her shirt. "This is about as far as I ever get. I'm surprised he didn't send the cops."

She hears the hesitation in his voice. "Well, he didn't send me. He just told Sam not to worry, that you had this place on the beach to go to when you needed to get away."

"He said that?"

"Something like that."

She lifts her head, leans it back against the warm wood. "I want to go home," she says, "home" sticking in her throat like a chicken bone.

"Well, okay," he says, and starts to get up.

"No, I mean *home*, home. New York."

"Oh." His cast bangs the stand as he slides back down.

"How can I stay here?"

"But your family's here," he says, frowning, gouging out a splinter of wood from the rough deck with his thumbnail.

"Family? What family?"

"You've got a family, Liv. You've got your dad." He sounds disappointed in her that she doesn't know something so obvious.

"Yeah, *right*!"

He doesn't say anything for a minute, just keeps gouging at the wood. "Some kids don't have anybody, Liv. I mean, nobody!"

Slow shake of her head, and she sighs. "Give me a break, Brian Spinuchi."

"No," he says, dead serious in a way that is new to her, his brilliant blue eyes sharply focused on her face. "You don't deserve a break, Liv. This is crap. I'm sorry, but it's true. There *are* people, kids, without homes. And you *do* have a family. What do you think? a family has to have—what?"—he throws up his left hand—"two parents? Two kids, a boy and a girl? I've got three moms . . . well, sort of. Does that mean I don't have a real family?" He stops, eyes wide, his cheeks flushed.

"Three moms?"

"Sure! My dad got married three times. So what? They're great people, all the women he got married to. I guess I should have thrown a fit or something, right? Run away from home. Like you!"

"*Three* moms?"

"Yeah! So what? There's all kinds of families, Liv. Most kids I know only have a mom. But that's their *family!*"

"You're something else, Brian Spinuchi," Liv says with a reluctant grin, swept up in the passion of his caring.

"Well, so are you, Liv. You're a spoiled brat."

Her eyes quickly check his. "You're kidding, right? You're *kidding* . . ."

"Nope. Not really." He doesn't back down, his blue eyes steady and sad. "You're acting like one, anyway."

"Well, thanks a lot. You can leave now."

"Aw, Liv . . ."

"No, I mean it." She feels herself heating up, and that heat protects her from pain, from feeling. "Just do me one favor. Tell my dad you couldn't find me."

His eyes so sad, as if he can really feel what she's going through. But how can he? "Why, Liv? Why should I tell him that? So he'll worry? You really don't think he cares about you?"

"He cares about himself. Himself and his damned abalones! Get out of here, Spinach. Get out of here and leave me alone!"

Long after Spinuchi's gone, after she's thought about what he said, gotten angry all over again, argued with him some more in her mind—saying all the right things this time— she climbs down to the cooling sand. Meanwhile, somehow without her noticing, the blackest of black skies has filled with stars. She peels off her running shoes, leaves them on the sand, heads off down the beach, her heels sinking where the water has withdrawn, leaving cobwebs of bubbles behind. She's alone in the universe, and that's the truth. She might as well get used to it.

Worse than anything is what she could never say aloud, not to Spinuchi, not to anyone. She's her father's daughter, after all. When the going gets tough, she bails.

23

LIV FEELS QUEASY and lightheaded as she steps off the bus and gets her first glimpse of Santa Barbara High. It's old, the main building, anyway, which comes as a surprise. But compared to her New York City school, also old, SBHS doesn't appear to be, well, *serious*. It's only two stories and looks just like all the other movie-set buildings in town, the banks, the shops, the Mission. Red tile roof and all that. It's a theme. Maybe there are rules about what you're allowed to build. Can they make rules like that in a democracy?

She squares her shoulders and heads through the iron gate as if she belongs.

Clumps of kids pass, on foot, in cars and pickup trucks. Too many are blond. Too many of the guys could be Spinuchi, except for his curls. She tries not to let it matter that he didn't call to offer her a ride. Why should he? She told him to take a hike, so now she gets to take one.

Arms crossed, she waits for the bell to ring, trying not to

look out of place, weird, lost. She gets *the* glance from several girls, so quick you wouldn't catch it, unless you'd done the same thing yourself hundreds of times to girls at your old school. Her shoes are okay, as it turns out. Black penny loafers. There's no consistency about shoes here. Some of the kids even wear flip-flops with Velcro straps. Strange. She could have worn her lizard boots, except that it's hot. No Santa Ana winds now, but still too hot for the beginning of a school year.

The bell rings and she joins the parade of bodies crushing through the double doors with that first day's sense of anticipation that never lasts. Lockers clang—you get to use them here, should she get one?—kids yell greetings the length of the long hallway. She's jostled several times, knocked around like a soccer ball. She's heart-thunking nervous, sweat beneath her nose. WELCOME BACK, say the green and gold letters of a banner. Liv checks her schedule once again to make sure she's looking for the right room. She finds A3 and goes immediately to the back, where three students are waiting for class to begin. Soon the room is filled with chatter and bodies. She feels invisible, hopes she is.

English lit, which could be a repeat of Mr. Denker's class. Piece of cake.

But when Mrs. Nelson comes through the door, Liv pulls out of her slouch. Tall and blond, Mrs. Nelson commands the room without seeming to try. Like a captain on deck. She begins to call the roll, solemnly greeting an occasional former student.

A titter crisscrosses the room. Mrs. Nelson looks up from the roll sheet toward the door. Liv's breath catches as she sees the golden curls, then the girl Spinuchi leaves at the door with a flash of his famous smile.

"You're late, Erica," Mrs. Nelson says. "If you're going to be in my class again, you will have to get here before the bell."

"Sorry, Mrs. Nelson!" Erica sings. She's got dimples in both cheeks, as if she's never done a thing in her entire life but giggle. Her coppery brown hair swirls and shifts against her back as she strolls to a seat on the far side of the room.

Liv's heart hurts. She feels it curling up inside, like a fist, like a hurt animal. Can it be true that all this time there was this . . . this *Erica*! It can't be, can it? Could a guy kiss like Spinuchi kissed her that day at the pond if he had an Erica in his life?

She hears her name from a long way off and doesn't answer. Mrs. Nelson's voice breaks through the fog. "Olivia Trager?"

"Here," Liv says, her voice cracking the word in half.

Mrs. Nelson gives her a sharp look over the top of her glasses, then goes on reading the roll.

If Spinuchi had a girlfriend, why did he kiss her, Miss Plain Jane Olivia Trager, that day at the pond? Why did he take her to feed the stupid ducks? Is that where he takes Erica? Maybe he takes lots of girls there. Like it's a cute thing to do and he knows it.

Stupid ducks, stupid girls.

It was just a stupid kiss. Well, a couple of stupid kisses. She made too big a deal out of it, that's all.

Except that he did, too. Didn't he? His eyes said he did. Well, maybe she can't read eyes like Gran can. Could.

Mrs. Nelson begins reading a poem in some strange-sounding language. Liv realizes she'd better start paying attention. Turns out the language is Old English, which Liv's at least heard of. Mrs. Nelson writes vowels on the board, asks the class to repeat their sounds. When she reads the poem again, *The Wanderer* it's called, Liv is so caught up in the rhythm of the language and the story that she forgets her pain for a while.

It returns hard at the end of the period as she catches a glimpse of golden curls at the other end of the hall. Spinuchi is laughing, his hands shaping what appears to be a very funny story. Erica shakes her hair back, laughing up at him—but wait! It's not Erica. It's another girl with dark swirling hair, this one is taller, broad-shouldered, a swimmer like her dad, maybe . . .

California girls are all so beautiful, so self-assured. How can she find her place here?

As the passing parade dodges around her, Liv catches herself staring, her mouth open and slack. Blushing, furious with herself, she turns and lets the crowd jostle her to the other end of the hall, then out into the courtyard into the glare of the sun, away from Spinuchi, away from Spinuchi and all his girlfriends.

The rest of the day passes in a blur of equations, irregular verbs, banging lockers. Liv carries herself from class to class, then onto the bus, like she's been wounded on the battlefield and patched together with a glue stick and string.

At home she crawls into a corner of the old brown couch and, drained, drops into sleep.

"Liv? You sick?" Her father leans down, peering into her face.

"Nope." She sits up, rubs the sleep from her face.

"Well then, cook us up these bugs, will you?" He hands her his pail. "I'm going over to pay the rent, and if I can get out of there without fixing a sink or toilet, I'll be back in a couple of minutes."

Liv stands, the pail hanging from her hand. "Wait!"

He turns, one hand on the doorknob.

"You want me to *kill* these lobsters?"

"No," he says in his maddeningly patient voice. "I want you to cook us up some dinner."

"Oh come on, Dad—" The two small lobsters thrash their tails in a vain attempt to escape what they probably guess is their fate.

"Don't make such a big damned deal of it, Liv. Just boil some water and drop them in."

And she gets an inspiration. "I'll do it on one condition," she says. "If you'll take me diving." She hears her words giving shape to the plan that's been growing in her mind. Payback.

"What do you mean?" Hands on his hips. "I said no diving on school days. And I'm taking the kid on Saturday. You know that."

"Take me instead."

Her father frowns, but the frown is tempered by the look in his eyes, which could be pride. *If* he were another kind of father, the kind that loves his kids and is proud of what they do, which is of course not the kind he is. "You like it, don't you? Tending. Being out there."

She shrugs. "Yeah."

"But I told the kid—"

"*I'm* your kid. I get first chance. Don't I?"

"Well, I suppose." He scratches the back of his neck, agitated. She's making things hard for him again. Just by being alive, she makes things hard for him. But isn't that what kids are for?

"Well, yeah, okay. You're on. Now make us some dinner."

Liv takes out the hot plate and plugs it in, sets the pot of water on it. When the water reaches a rolling boil, she grabs one of the lobsters, then the other one, the way her father has shown her. "In you go, Erica," she says. "In you go, Brian Spinuchi."

Still, it doesn't feel exactly good to have killed.

Day two begins. All that holds Liv together is the thought that it *had* to get better. It couldn't get worse.

"Hey!"

She turns at the sound of the familiar voice, the touch on her shoulder. Spinuchi. He seems to have gotten taller, older. Or maybe just farther away.

"Oh, hi," she says flatly. But the heat in her cheeks has got to be giving her away.

"I've been looking all over for you!" Same sweet smile. "How was your first day? Do you like the school?" He's got two arms. He had two arms yesterday, too, she realizes now. But all she could see yesterday was Erica, Spinuchi and Erica, Spinuchi and that other one . . .

"Sure. It's fine. Hey, I gotta go! My French class is all the way over in one of those outbuildings."

Spinuchi looks a little knocked back. "I can do anything. I mean, you know, tell you anything about the school, or—" But she sails off down the hall with a Miss Teen America wave. "Glad you got your cast off! See ya!"

"Yeah . . . see ya." She senses that he hasn't moved. That his mouth is hanging open and his eyes are bugging out, just like hers were the day before. Or anyway, it's what she hopes. She doesn't dare look back.

Wait till her father tells Spinuchi he's not taking him diving this weekend. Mr. Sweetness won't be smiling then!

But inside, she's aching again. Her life seems to be all about loss. She might as well figure out how to deal with it. Grow a tough shell, like an abalone. Like a father.

24

BANG. BANG. BANG. "Time to get up! Liv! Get up!"

Bang. Bang. Bang. The door rattles, loose on its hinges. Rattles her head, dumb with sleep.

Liv stumbles out of bed and into her clothes before her mind can begin to sort out what she's doing. Saturday. No school. Tending. Taking Spinuchi's job, which seemed like a great idea just yesterday. Now all she can think about is how cold the wind can be, how long a day at sea really is.

Her father has made coffee with the coffeepot, a surprise. There's an ashtray on the table, a lipstick-tipped butt crushed into it, an even bigger surprise. Sam must have come over after Liv went to bed. Did her father actually let Sam smoke inside? And why is Sam still smoking?

Sam.

She won't think about Sam. Or about how she ran out on Sam, what a jerk she was and continues to be.

"Make us a couple of sandwiches, will you?"

Her father gulps his coffee, rinses out what's left of it, washes the cup, dries it, sets it back in the cupboard. If he weren't a diver, he'd be a chemist. Or a librarian. All that precision, and for nothing. She asked him once why he never went to college. What he needed to know they didn't teach in college, he said. But it wasn't true.

"You got a real heavy hand with the mayo, you know that?"

"No, Father," Liv says. "I did not know that."

"Don't be a smart ass," he says.

The harbor is enveloped in a thick gray fog. By the time they get to the *Jeannie T* Liv is damp and shivering. She wraps herself in Spinuchi's jacket and, like a robot, follows the orders her father barks at her. It won't be long, she tells herself. She won't be doing this for long. As soon as she can save enough for plane fare and a little more, she's out of here. Spinuchi's just one more reason to go. Not the main reason. The main reason owns this boat. She knows *he* won't care if she goes back to New York, not really. Oh, he'll make a big fuss. Because he knows that's what fathers are supposed to do. But once she's gone, he'll be relieved.

When he's satisfied that everything has been taken care of, her father cranks the engine. It starts up, dies. He cranks it again. "Damn," he says, as it fails a second time. "Hope that's not the carburetor." On the third try, the engine catches and he backs the boat out of the slip, frowning. He listens to the rumble of the engine with everything that is in him; Liv can see this in the way he stands or moves.

On the horizon a faint pink line expands, and then, like a curtain rising, the fog lifts, revealing pale blue sky.

As they idle out of the harbor, Liv looks back, even though she can't see Sam's boat from where they are.

She thinks about asking her father about Sam, if Sam said anything about Liv bolting like a spooked rabbit out of the apartment, and if she's upset. Maybe even mad at Liv. But Liv knows better than to ask her father questions like that. About abalones, the ocean, boats, she can ask him anything and he'll tell her all he knows and more. But when it comes to questions about people, about . . . *life!* he's hopeless.

"I'm going back to New York," she says. To get it over with, to get the words out of her.

His surprise surprises her. "Why?" he asks, not barking this time. Can it be that he really doesn't know, doesn't understand why she would want to leave?

She feels the hot threat of tears in her throat. "I don't know . . ." and for a minute she really doesn't know. New York isn't home anymore, not now that Gran is gone. Suds writes about new friends, and Megan seldom writes at all. If Liv hadn't gone to that stupid private school all those years, she'd have had more high school friends. If she tries hard enough, she can blame Emma Woods for everything. "I just don't belong here."

"Well, that's where you're wrong," he says. "Until you're

eighteen years of age, this is exactly where you do belong. I told you that before." The engine idles, occasionally skipping. She can see on his face the effort it takes for him to listen, half to the engine, half to her. "You gotta give it time, Liv."

"What?" she asks. "Give what time?"

Gripping the wheel, he squints into the distance. "You ask too many questions! Do you think I know everything? You know you have to give it time."

"What? Give *what* time?"

He throws up his hands, exasperated. "California!" he says, as if it should be obvious to her.

"Oh," she says, heart aching. "I thought maybe you meant, like, us." She looks down at her shredded sneakers, blinking back tears.

He gives her a blank look. "Us?"

"Yeah . . ." She wipes her sleeve across her eyes, looks away from him, from his puzzled expression, out at the islands that seem to float unattached between fog and sky. "Yeah, you and me."

She can tell he's thinking, or maybe he's just listening to the engine. His forehead is furled, but his eyes are unreadable.

While her father dives, Liv writes to Sam, apologizing, trying to explain why she ran out, why she hasn't returned Sam's calls. But when she reads the letter over, her words sound childish and dumb. Besides, a letter is just another way to avoid facing Sam in person, to avoid telling her that she, Liv, can't be counted on. She balls up the letter, stuffs it into her backpack.

The hose jerks and Liv pulls her father in. He surfaces with his bag nearly empty. He climbs into the boat like an old man, bent over and complaining. Four dives and only ten snots.

After lunch he goes back down. "I'll be damned if I'm going back with less than three dozen," he grumbles. But he finds a good spot by midafternoon and is in high spirits again. "You gotta see this reef," he says. "Why don't you get into Spinuchi's suit again. I'll take you down."

"Diving? Like *under* the water?"

"Sure. Yeah."

"Not just like . . . snorkeling."

"Nah. That's for sissies."

With nervous excitement she changes clothes in the cabin. If she had worn a bathing suit, all this would be easier. But it doesn't matter now. She won't be his tender for long.

She watches while he switches something on the compressor and adds another hose.

He mutters, "This is all the tenders want to do, you know. They don't want to tend. They just want to know how to get the abs, then they quit and get their boat and become more competition for me."

They do the spitting thing with their masks. "Here's your regulator," he says, handing her a round plastic disk with a mouthpiece on it. "Don't hold your breath, dummy. Breathe." She breathes the air in and out, her heart hammering so hard she can hear it. Is this something she wants to do? Is she doing it just to please him? Will she die trying to please him? Does it matter?

"Spinuchi's fins will probably fit you," he yells as if she's gone deaf. He hands her the fins, adjusts the weight on Spinuchi's weight belt, and gives that to her, too. After tightening the straps on the fins, she's ready.

Her father slips neatly into the water and instructs her from there. "Okay, now sit on the side just like before, that's it. Now swing your legs over and just slide in. Like I did."

Liv doesn't give herself time to think about it. She takes a deep breath, drops into the water beside her father. "Now, the thing is not to panic. Understand? It's only twenty-thirty feet. You're going to go down just like you went after those pennies at the YMCA pool."

She nods, clutching fearfully to the side of the boat.

He pulls on his mask and holds out his hand. "There's nothing to worry about, Liv," he says. "I've got you." For a moment their eyes meet through the water-spotted lenses of their masks.

Even with the weight belt, her wet suit wants to keep her on the surface and it's hard to dive. She tries it several times, her butt bobbing on the surface. Finally, it works and she goes under, still clutching his hand.

They dive together, down, down, through sun-filtered

water, yellowy brown dust, his fins propelling them into brilliant blue light, patches of shadow. Directly below a school of a billion small silver fish. She squeezes her father's hand, points. He nods. This is a world without words, no wonder he's so comfortable in it. The silver fish change direction, all at once and instantly, almost faster than the eye can follow, and are gone. Sea fans wave up from a weedy reef. From here, the thick forest of kelp twirls up and up, reaching for light.

Liv can feel her heart tripping, echoing in her ears. She's terrified, but at the same time completely captivated by this underwater world in which she's never been. After a while, gliding next to her father, the terror fades and she's at peace for the first time since Gran died. It's almost as if this is where she belongs, her body remembering the feeling from an earlier time, from a time long before she was born. Or the time right before birth when she floated inside her mother, tethered but free.

They skim the smooth bottom, then rise above a long, narrow reef. Her father turns, puts a finger up to say, "One minute," and lets go of her hand. Too fascinated to be afraid, as afraid as she knows she should be, Liv does her best to stay in place, clumsy now that he's no longer guiding her. Waving her hands, bicycling her feet, she watches him.

For several minutes he hovers above the reef, his abalone iron in his right hand. Then he drops quickly and pokes his iron at the ledge, under the shell of an abalone she doesn't even see until he's got it in his hand. He claps it onto his chest, comes back, and takes her hand again. She gives him a grin and a thumbs-up. His eyes crinkle, so she can tell he's smiling. Underwater, he can smile. He points up. Directly above, a school of silvery brown fish like fat little trucks chugging along.

Her breathing comes more easily now, but still she clutches hard on to his rough hand. He takes them cruising along the reef, pointing at things she sometimes doesn't see. Fish go in and out of holes and ledges, busy in pursuit of food or each other. Some are curious enough to come straight up to her mask and look in. When she laughs, her voice hollows out through the hose.

Her father is like a fish himself, stopping on a dime, swimming without seeming to try. This time when he lets her go, she mimics the back-and-forth motion he makes with his hands that keep him in place. He nudges his iron at the bottom, and Liv's heart flips over as a pair of huge wings rise out of the silt. The ray flutters off, hardly perturbed. Her father turns his mask to her and she can see he's enjoying himself, this show he's putting on for her. She pats her heart, widens her eyes. His eyes crinkle.

After a while he points to the surface to ask if she's had enough. She shakes her head emphatically. So he pulls her around some more, sometimes stopping, poking around while she hovers above, learning to be easy on her own, the way a child learns to let go and take her first steps. He's never far from her.

A long, dark shadow passes overhead. Her father looks up. Rising quickly, he grabs for her hand. This time he tucks her whole arm under his and they ascend, fast, through the silty water, through their bubbles, back up to the blue light, his fins moving powerfully. They break the surface at the back of the boat. He yanks off his mask. "Climb up," he orders, pushing on her back, almost lifting her out of the water. She clambers up onto the outdrive, stumbles into the boat. He's right behind her.

"Wow! That was fast!" She's elated, pumped full of adrenaline. "Why did we come up so fast? Won't we get the bends?"

"Not deep enough," he says. She knows he saw something down there by the way he brought them up. He cuts the compressor, tidies up, putting away the extra hose and mask, avoiding her eyes.

"That was cool, Dad," she says. "I loved it!"

"Yeah, I figured," he says grimly. "There goes another tender!" But she can tell he's kidding, she's beginning to know that much about him.

She bends her head to get the water out of her right ear. "Can we do this again sometime? Will you take me down again?"

"I thought you were going back to New York." He says this mockingly, as if no one in their right mind would ever go to New York. "Maybe you can get somebody to take you diving there. You can dive for garbage in New York Harbor!" He chuckles to himself, shaking his head as he reaches for the key. "Put the life jacket on." The engine coughs and dies. "Damn," he says, and tries again, but the engine won't start. He pulls the hatch to the engine, pokes around inside, muttering "Fuel filter," then "Damned carburetor . . ."

The fog has been drifting in, soft wisps at first, a veil in the air between the ocean and the sun. Her father has taken out his tools. "Hard to predict these things," he says to himself. "Damned fog's moving in."

Liv munches on cookies, voracious. She's warm inside the wet suit, but the fog chills her spirits. As her father works, the sky begins to darken, the sun a pale white disk that appears and disappears in the fog and finally sets in a gray gloom. "Okay," he says at last. "Okay." He replaces the hatch. "Didn't I tell you to put the running lights on?" He stomps across the deck. A red and a green light appear on either side of the bow. He's agitated, more than she's ever seen.

"Is it fixed?" she asks. "Did you fix it?"

"Yeah, yeah," he says. The engine turns over, idling smoothly. "It's just that it's so damned late." He glances around with worried eyes. "We shouldn't be out here."

"Why?"

"Think about it, Liv. We can't see five feet in front of us. Do you think anybody can see *us*?"

"Who?" she scoffs. "There's nobody out here." But she's trembling just the same.

"Let's hope not," he says tightly. "Keep your eyes open

and listen. Listen like you've never listened in your life. If you hear something—anything—get ready to dive over the side. Understand?"

Liv stares into the fog, her face streaming wet. Her father leans forward over the wheel, as if that will help him see. Sam says he "can't see the back end of a barn," but he won't get his eyes checked.

Sam. Liv can't wait to tell Sam all about her first real dive. Then she will apologize. It's about time. The *Jeannie T* rumbles steadily through the dark water. A feeling that she is a true part of all this, or that all of this has become a permanent part of her, takes away her apprehension, the way Gran's hand once smoothed the worry from her forehead. It won't be long before they spot the oil rigs and the lights of the harbor.

"The other night when I took off?" The fog makes it easier for her to talk to her father, as if they're in a separate world, or a new world beginning.

"Yeah?"

"It was stupid. I just . . . freaked, I guess. I couldn't stand to think about what could happen to Sam, that she could just . . . die. Like Gran. Like my mother."

"I know," he says. "I know that."

"You do?"

"Isn't that what I was telling you? That day, in the kitchen, you remember. You asked why I left you. It wasn't right, I know that, Liv. Believe it or not, I'm not exactly a moron. But I was scared. Scared shitless. I'd already screwed up so bad—" He stops, listens, his dark eyes wide. "Did you hear that?"

They both strain to listen. A dull thrumming sound in the distance. Behind them? In front of them?

Then a shape, dark, immense, looms out of the fog.

It is the last thing Liv remembers.

25

AT FIRST NOTHING IS CLEAR, nothing real. As she bobs in the dark water, Liv's mind just names the things she sees: hose like an undulating snake; glove, its fingers stiff and curled; plastic bread wrapper; gull riding a broken board.

Liv yells for her father, her voice hollowing out into the darkness. Frantically she turns circles, her arms flapping. "Dad! Dad!" How often she stopped short of granting him that name. My *father*, she'd say, not Dad. My *father*. Because he gave her life, and nothing more. "Dad!" she yells over and over, until she grows hoarse. He tried to be more, she knows that. But she wouldn't let him. She wanted to make him pay and pay.

"Dad! Help, Dad!" She starts to swim, breaststroke, in one direction, then another. "Dad! Dad! Where are you?" The sea mocks her with its rolling silence. In her mind Liv sees the dark shape of the boat that hit the *Jeannie T*, tries to recapture the sound of what must have been a horrendous crash, tries to remember how she got into the water—did she leap as her father told her to? Did he? But if he did, if he made it, wouldn't he be somewhere near? She calls and calls him until her throat is dry and sore.

After a while it becomes obvious that crying isn't going to save her life, so Liv begins to think of what might. She's a strong swimmer; the life vest keeps her buoyant; there's debris around her everywhere, maybe something she can cling to. She pushes through the mess, looking for something to help keep her afloat. The cooler lid is a gift, bobbing within easy reach. She grabs it, resting her arms. Then the current pulls her away and she leaves what's left of the *Jeannie T* in her wake.

Can she save herself? There is too much she doesn't know. Is she in a shipping lane? Can the wreck be seen from the air? What happened to the boat that hit them? Where is the current taking her? She remembers her father saying there is nothing between this coast and the coast of Japan. If she keeps on going, will she end up there? Keeping her mind busy with questions holds the panic at bay.

How long could a person last in the Pacific Ocean? She'd need water, fresh water, that she knows. She will die in a few days without water.

If she lasts a few days. In her wet suit she looks like a seal. There are sharks. Her whole body contracts in fear at the thought of them. Her father said to punch a shark in the nose and it might go away. The thought of doing that makes her giggle, and a bubble of hysteria rises inside her. She swallows it.

Keep calm, keep calm, keep calm.

Looking up, she searches through dispersing fog for signs of a plane, running lights, though she knows she will never be spotted in the dark. A three-quarter moon floats in a black sky empty of stars. On the water, moon-ripples like white silk. That she can see beauty, still see that something so terrifying as the night ocean could still be beautiful, amazes her. She tries to keep the spirit of her grandmother with her. *What now, Gran? If the going gets wet, do the wet keep going? If life gives you salt water . . .*

Oh, Gran, what now?

It isn't surprising that Gran doesn't answer, it doesn't mean she isn't listening. At the end of the day, when Liv was still wired from school, still full of stories to tell, Gran, weary, would close her eyes to listen. She said she could hear better that way. Now, as then, Liv goes right on talking.

In the dark Liv has no idea which way to go, to swim. She cannot see the shore, the hills. Every direction she turns in looks the same. Gran once told her, when she was very young, that if she got lost, all she had to do was stand still, right where she was, and somebody would find her. It happened once in Macy's. Gran was right. But Liv can't stay still, the current won't let her.

Clinging to her cooler lid, she bobs in the deep black water like a rubber doll, riding the current. Disconnected thoughts swim through and out of her mind, like fish in a reef. The cooler lid, bright blue, looks inky in the dark. Spinuchi's eyes are blue. Liv has her father's eyes. She has some of his fears, too, but it's what Gran has given her that keeps her afloat. Sam has cancer. Liv is a spoiled brat. Who cares if there's an Erica? Spinuchi's eyes are the bluest blue . . .

After a while, shoulders aching from her death grip on the cooler lid, Liv rolls onto her back, threading her arms under the lid and resting her head. Her fingers are shriveled, her feet numb.

A wave of exhaustion seeps through her, but Liv fights to stay awake, to hang on to the cooler lid. Without it, she knows she can't last. She is strong, but not strong enough for this, for challenging the sea.

Keep calm, keep calm, keep calm . . .

She begins to hum, then to sing. Suds always laughs at her for knowing all the "stupid elevator songs," but they are the songs she and Gran sang when they cleaned house, and they buoy her spirits now. Songs from Fred Astaire movies or Broadway show tunes. Gran, dusting the bookshelves, her hair wrapped in an Aunt Jemima scarf, warbled lines from "I'm Gonna Wash That Man Right Outa My Hair." There never was a man, though, not after Grandpa. And yet it never occurred to Liv that she didn't have a "real" family, not once in all those fifteen years.

Sam and Liv painting the walls peach, Sam belting out sixties tunes. Gran and Sam so much alike. Of course Liv was afraid to lose her, that made perfect sense. But running away didn't help. It seems so clear to her now: you couldn't outrun your fears, you had to ride them out.

"Younger than springtime . . ." sings Liv, riding the swell.

When she was a child, she would sing in the bathtub with her ears underwater. She would plink the keys of a pretend piano on the bubbled surface.

Gran's brother, the youngest one, drowned in a catfish pond only four feet deep. Water was the enemy. And yet, just this morning, gliding through it at her father's side, something had come alive in her. She had found something.

"Dad! Dad!" Is her father floating, too, somewhere between here and Japan? Maybe he's alive. But her voice comes back to her each time disembodied, a lonely echo of itself. The black water dips and rolls around her.

It's sad, but if Liv doesn't make it, Sam will never know how sorry she was.

Is.

Present tense, past tense; crossing the line between life and death; Liv's mother, Gran, and now Liv herself.

If Liv's father is gone, too, Sam will be all alone. All that worry about losing Sam, and now Sam has lost them.

Is this an irony, Mr. Denker?

At the thought of her old teacher, a phrase from a Yeats poem pops into Liv's head. ". . . the foul rag-and-bone shop of the heart." She liked that line as soon as she read it, though she hadn't a clue what it meant. Mr. Denker did, though, he always did. But of course, he wouldn't tell the class, leading them on instead like a game-show host. "What *images* come to mind? What do you *see*?"

"My dad's garage!" Guffaws from the rest of the jocks at the back of the room.

"A cemetery?" suggested Suds. Suds is a very literal person.

The discussion had gone on and on, until even Liv had grown weary of it. But now she knows what the words mean. She would tell Mr. Denker if only she could, because Liv's father had a rag-and-bone shop for a heart. It didn't make him a bad person. His heart was just filled with sadness, old fears. He wasn't the Tin Man, after all. He had a heart; it was just filled with old junk.

The nudge comes when she has stopped thinking, when her mind is in a kind of zone and she is nothing but body, nothing but a drifting body. Something bumps her right thigh and moves on. Instantly awake, filled with panic, Liv freezes, her senses alert and screaming. In her mind she sees the shark, waits for its return. She begins to sob, the way the victims always sob in slasher movies when they know Freddy Krueger is somewhere in the house, the sob of the helpless.

A second nudge. The ghost of a silvery shape in the water. Dolphin! She has to see, has to know. She can't wait for it—shark or dolphin—to come to her. She puts her face in the water, opens her eyes, and there it is, looking back at her with its comical Flipper face.

The night wears on. Liv drifts again and again near the dangerous shores of sleep. So cold, so cold . . . But if she closes her eyes, the dolphin appears again at her side, nudging her awake. Once, it lets her sleep and she dreams she is riding its back.

Or it is a dream, no dolphin at all, only Gran's strength in arms that grip the cooler lid, even in sleep.

Toward morning, when the sky begins to gray and the surface of the water is slick and oily-looking, she begins to babble, saying stupid things, dreaming with her eyes open, talking to the dolphin that she is not sure was ever really there; talking with Gran, with Sam, with her father and Spinuchi, as if they are all old friends gathered at a swim party.

Her mouth is sticky with thirst, and the thought sneaks in in spite of her: she will never be found. She cannot control the chattering of her teeth. How easy it would be to slide off the cooler lid, to just let go.

Virginia Woolf, that's who it was. That's who stuck the rocks in her pocket. Ten points for that.

Then the sun begins to rise, the slightest trace of faint pink gold on the gray horizon. Liv rides up a steep swell and sees, at the top, in the graying light of morning, how immense, how terrifyingly immense the ocean is. She tries to take it in, what that means. What such immensity means to her hopes for rescue. Hollowed out inside, empty, she knows now that it is hopeless. She will never be found.

As the sun climbs the sky, the swell builds. Liv is swept up the moving wall of water and down the other side, as if she is just one more piece of ocean debris. Her mind drifts easily now, dangerously. She has drifted to a place beyond words, beyond thoughts, when she hears a buzzing sound above her. She jerks up her head, blinks to clear the salty water from her eyes.

At first it is no more than a dot in the sky, then a cross. But it's a plane, a small plane! It flies low, straight toward her, a small red-and-white plane with black writing. Numbers. A 4, then an 8. No, it's an H. Is she dreaming? She screams and waves her arms, grabs back the cooler lid. The plane crosses straight across the sun. It passes without a sign that it has spotted her. "Oh, God," she cries. "Oh, God, no! Come back!" She starts to sob, dry hoarse sobs.

She is a speck, less than a speck. How could she possibly be spotted? She has to make herself more visible. Somehow. But how?

She lays her head on the cooler lid, closes her eyes, and, for the first time, tries to pray. It is more a plea for life than a prayer, a plea to the God of her childhood, the now-I-lay-me-down-to-sleep God that she'd lost touch with, thought she had no need for. Religion was like everything else in Gran's life, something to explore, to savor, to learn from. Gran herself was a "transcendentalist," like Emerson and Thoreau. God was everywhere in nature, in fact *was* nature. But she and Liv visited many houses of God in Liv's lifetime: churches, synagogues, attended gospel services in tenement basements. Liv would find her own way, Gran said, in her own good time.

Well, it was probably time.

She is almost afraid to believe it when she hears the engine a second time. She scans the nearly white sky, squint-ing into the sun. This time she's got to be seen! She searches the water, as if there's something, anything, she can grab up and wave. But there's nothing but blue-black water. Then it hits her. The bright red lining of Spinuchi's wet suit! Maybe it can be seen if she can't. She knows the danger of taking off the life vest and jacket, but it is her only hope. As the plane comes into view, flying low, she struggles out of the jacket, frantically turns it inside out, and waves it slowly through the water. "Here!" she cries, her teeth chattering. "I'm here! Oh, God, please, I'm here!"

The plane flies straight overhead. But its wings dip once, then twice, before it flies on.

26

WHITE BANDAGE. Clear plastic tube snaking up through a dazzle of sunshine. Outside a window, gnarled branches of an ancient tree. Bed rail, the whitest sheets. All this is somehow connected to her.

Hospital. Where is Gran? Gran is gone. But wasn't Gran just sitting on the side of her bed holding her hand? Wasn't Gran right there whenever she awoke and then fell away again, off the edge into something that felt much deeper than sleep?

"Pretty as your mama, tough as your dad," said Gran, her voice ghosting away into darkness.

Liv blinks now to make sure she's awake. Needles of pain in her head. Memory returns in flashes, as if her mind knows just how much she can take at one time. *Cross in the sky, the wings of a plane, black water, a wall of water that she rode to the top, a blue cooler lid . . .*

Her stomach lurches. Liv rolls just in time to spill watery

liquid onto the polished tile floor. Splat, and then the dry heaving when nothing else follows. Seasick again, this time on land.

Fog, thick gray fog, and then the ship!

"Oh my Lord, what happened here?" Dark face, darker freckles over a broad nose, sure hands that settle Liv back against her pillows and smooth the sheets. "I left the room for . . . *what?*"—eyebrows shoot up and the nurse checks her watch—"a whole five minutes. You okay now? I'll get you something to calm your stomach." She dabs Liv's face with a cool damp cloth. Liv wants to ask a million questions, but her stomach says to hold still, very still.

The nurse is still talking, a running string of conversation that demands nothing in return. ". . . never left your side, couldn't get him to go for a bite or nothing! *Stubborn.* Telling everybody their business, what the doctor needed to do for hypothermia, and this and that— Well, you were just a little dehydrated, that's all, no hypothermia. What a time you had, sugah! All over the newspaper, too, wait'll you see. You're famous. Anyway, I finally got him to leave so that I could clean you up a bit. That was just a while ago, do you remember that? I 'spect he'll be here again momentarily."

"My head hurts," Liv manages.

"Getcha something for that, too. You just rest, hear? That's what you need."

Liv gets a glimpse of kinky copper-red hair. Sam at the door peering in. Behind Sam, her father. Spinuchi, too. Red roses in a huge bouquet.

"Come in, come on in. Can't stop you anyway, no regular visitor hours here, the Lord only knows why." The nurse sighs, pats Liv's hand. "I'll get you those meds now, girl. These folks wear you out, you just press that button, hear?"

Liv attempts a smile.

They gather around her bed, long-faced and solemn, as if she's dead. They talk in quiet voices. Spinuchi's eyes are wide and worried, Sam keeps blinking back tears; her father clears his throat as if he's about to speak, but nothing comes out.

"How do you feel, sweetie?" Sam says at last. "You slept so long, we thought you were never going to wake up!"

"I'm fine," Liv says. Seeing Sam after what seems like forever fills Liv's eyes with tears. "I'm sorry, Sam."

"For what, sweetie?" Sam looks puzzled.

"For running out. You know—"

"Hey, you were worried about me! I know that. But how are *you* doing? Are you feeling okay?"

"Yeah. I mean, I think so. Why am I here? What's wrong with me?"

"Precaution," her father spouts. His big arms crossed, he stands slightly behind Sam. "Nothing wrong with you. They checked you all out, blood, urine, the works. You surprised 'em. Well, I said you'd have lasted a lot longer if you had to, strong girl like you . . ." He sounds upset, angry. At the doctors? At her? Did she do something wrong, and is that why all this happened? She can't remember much. Mostly just the water, rolling black water that went on and on forever.

"Hi, Spinuchi," she says, offering him her free hand. She's so happy to see him, she doesn't care that he knows it, that he already has a girlfriend or two. Something has changed inside her, she doesn't know exactly what. It feels as if she's dropped something dark and heavy behind her, or simply let it go because it weighed too much. "Thanks for the wet suit."

He grins. "Don't mention it."

"They really are just being careful," Sam assures Liv. "One more night, the doctor says, then you can come home."

"No reason she can't just come home right now!" her father fumes, his neck and cheeks dark red. "You feel fine, don't you, Liv?"

"Well, yeah, I . . ."

Sam puts a hand on Liv's father's arm. "Calm down, honey. The doctors know what they're doing. What can we bring you, Liv? Magazines? Chocolate? I'll bring a change of clothes tomorrow, okay?"

Liv smiles, nods. A wave of exhaustion makes her eyelids drop.

"We'll let you rest now," says Sam. "I haven't been able to get your father to lea—"

"Never mind, never mind," he says, shushing her. "Okay, then. You sleep, Liv. That's the thing to do. One more night, but that's it." He frowns at Spinuchi. "Well, let's go, then. Liv needs her rest!"

Spinuchi grins at Liv, rolls his eyes as if to say, *There he goes again.* Sam herds Liv's protesting father out the door. "Come on, Mark. Leave the kids alone for a minute."

Spinuchi stares at Liv, still wide-eyed, as if she's come back from the dead. "Wow, Liv, I don't know what to say. When the report came in at the Harbor Master's—"

"You were there?"

"Yeah! I was on one of the boats that went out. Are you okay? I mean, really?"

"I guess so. I mean, I feel . . . normal." She tries to read in his gaze how bad she must look with her puffy, chapped lips and seaweed hair.

"Well, you look normal." He shrugs, embarrassed.

Then neither of them seems to know what to say next.

"Your father's too much," Spinuchi says, grabbing at a topic they both find endlessly amusing. "You should have seen him buying the flowers. It's like he knew what all the colors were for, only he couldn't keep them straight, what color was for what. He drove us crazy. I told him you had to have the red ones, because they were the nicest." He shrugs. "Of course, he wouldn't let me buy them." He shakes his head. "Well, you know how he is . . ."

"I think I'm beginning to," Liv says, hearing in her words the quiet ring of truth.

"Look, Liv . . ." Spinuchi perches carefully on the side of her bed, frowning. He carefully takes her hand, looks at it as if it's worth examining in great detail. "There's something I didn't tell you—"

"I know. It's okay." And because he's holding her hand, and because she's alive, it really is.

He turns to meet her gaze. "You know?"

"About Erica? Sure. I saw you two together the first day."

"Damn," he says, shaking his head. "I'm such a jerk."

"Yeah, you could have told me. Then I wouldn't have had to throw myself into the ocean!"

"You're kidding!"

"Brian Spinuchi, you are amazing. I guess girls kill themselves over you about every other week, right?"

"Damn, Liv, be serious. You scared the crap out of me!"

"Well, I meant to!"

"You shouldn't kid about things like that." Disappointed, he sets her hand down, gets up, stuffs his hands in his pockets. "Well, hey, I'm glad you're all right." Stubborn streak in those clear blue eyes.

"I'm sorry," she says contritely. "I guess I'm just trying to pay you back for not being straight with me."

He tries again: "Look, what I've been trying to say—"

"Yeah?"

"—is that, well, Erica isn't . . ." He stops, starts up again, sighs, shuffles his feet. "This is tough."

Liv's barely breathing. Erica isn't *what*?

"Erica isn't, well . . ."

Liv can't stand it any longer. "What? Erica isn't what? Rich? Smart? She sure isn't ugly."

Spinuchi laughs. "Erica isn't my, like, girlfriend. I guess that's what I'm trying to say."

"Huh." Exactly like her father.

"No, I mean it. When I saw her at school today? She's just this, this . . ."

Liv watches him struggling to find the right words. Part of her (the not-so-nice part) hopes he'll bad-mouth Erica, the other part (what Gran called her "better self") knowing she won't respect him nearly so much if he does.

"She's nice and all, don't get me wrong! But I'm not, well, ready to hang out with, well, just one person, I guess." He takes a chance and looks miserably into Liv's eyes. "I mean, if I was, *ready*—"

"I'm sorry, Spinuchi." Liv sighs.

"Yeah," he sighs. "Me, too." But he sounds relieved.

"No, it's not what you're thinking. I owe *you* an apology. When I saw you with Erica and . . . *whomever*, I decided to pay you back by taking your job away. Crummy, huh?"

He shrugs. "Guess I deserved it."

"No, you didn't. And besides, look who got paid back!"

"Whoa! That's right!" says Spinuchi, slapping his knee, always a beat behind. "Guess I'd be in the hospital right now instead of you!"

"So," says Liv. "Friends, right?" She holds out her hand. For a second Spinuchi looks as if he knows he's lost something he might care a whole lot about later on. "Friends," he says.

"Thanks for coming to see me," she says. "Thanks for the roses. Only they shouldn't have been red, you know."

"Huh? Why?"

"Oh, I'll tell you sometime." She tries to suppress a yawn and fails.

Liv drifts in and out of sleep the rest of the day. Several different nurses check her pulse, replace the IV bag, write things on her chart. A doctor comes in at the end of the day, shines a penlight into her eyes, feels the glands in her neck, checks her chart. "You had quite an ordeal," he says. "None the worse for wear, though. Good strong heart." He pats her shin and leaves.

When they bring her dinner, she eats every bit of it: stewed chicken, mashed potatoes, corn, green Jell-O, and it all stays down.

Then sleep overtakes her again, pulls her down into a warm, dry nest where she doesn't have to think about anything. She doesn't dream, so when she sees her father sitting on the chair next to her bed, she knows it is really him. She doesn't move; through the slits of her eyelids she studies the bulky shape of him. His head has fallen nearly to his chest, shoulders hunched forward, hands clasped and dropped between his thighs. She wonders how long he has been there, asleep, and how he manages not to topple forward onto the floor. Should she wake him? But then, as she watches, he wakes himself, jolts up, clearing his throat. She closes her eyes, feigns sleep.

She hears him sigh, then a sound as if he might be rubbing his hands over his face.

"Liv? You awake?"

She doesn't answer.

"That's okay, you sleep. That's the best thing." Several seconds pass, then almost inaudibly: "God, Liv, I am so sorry . . ."

She keeps her breathing even and shallow, but every bit of her is alert and listening.

"Your old man screwed up. Again. Well, hell . . . " He sighs. The plastic chair sighs as he shifts his weight. "You can't start over, that's the thing. Can't undo what you did before. Doesn't work that way . . ."

She nearly stops breathing when she hears the sobs. They have to be coming from him, though it's nearly impossible to believe. She opens her eyes. Her father's face is in his hands. His big shoulders heave. His sobs, muffled, go on and on.

She needs to say something, but what? Reaching as far as her arm will go, she touches his knee. "It's okay, Dad." It isn't much. It's all she can think of. She means so much more.

His face comes up out of his hands. He looks frightened at first, as if she's caught him doing something shameful. Then he grabs a wad of tissues from the bedside table, blows his nose. Won't look at her now. "Guess it's all caught up with me," he says, as if there's something outside himself to blame, some disease of the mind or heart.

"It wasn't your fault," she says. "It was an accident."

He is quiet for several minutes, looking at her, but through her, too, as if he's gone into some other time and place. "There are all kinds of accidents, Liv. What we call accidents. You asked me on the boat if your mama and I, well . . . if your mother and I ever talked about having a child. Well, we did. Just a couple of kids ourselves, you know . . . but we did. We talked about all that. How she wanted a boy that looked like me, how I wanted a girl just like her—" He grins sheepishly. "You know, the way you do when, well, when you're crazy about somebody." He breaks off, looks down at his hands, rubs away at a knuckle. "I didn't think it could really happen, that her heart would just . . . give! And then when they handed you to me! God, what a *weight*!" He laughs, shortly. "You were too real for me, kiddo. Hollering, waving your fists like you wanted to punch somebody out. Ha!" He runs his fingers back through his hair. "Never been so scared in all my life. So when your grandmother offered to take you—for a while, she said, until I got myself together—well, I told myself it was the best thing. For *you*. Yeah, well . . ." He ducks his head, studies the palm of his right hand. "Then a while became a longer while, and then—well, you know the rest . . ."

"Yeah," Liv says softly.

"And then yesterday, all those hours when I thought, well, that you were gone!" His dark eyes widen, remembering. "All I could think of was that damned carburetor and how I should've checked it more carefully. That was when I figured it all out, you see. The thing is, I'd been given this . . . this second chance, you know, with *you*. And I blew it again." He stops, winded, as if he's run a word marathon and worn himself out.

"You didn't blow it, Dad. *We* didn't blow it. It's all right. It's all right now." Funny, how she'd always wanted his comfort, proof of his love, and how good it feels to be comforting him. Her hand rests on his knee; his hand lightly on her hand, light as a breath, but there.

27

THE STORY WAS FRONT-PAGE NEWS: TEEN SUR-
VIVES WRECK AT SEA. Her father had been picked up almost
immediately, the article said, by the oil tanker that had wan-
dered out of the shipping lane and hit the small dive boat.
The *Tidewater II* had crisscrossed the sea in every direction,
her father aboard calling her name. By then, they had ra-
dioed the Coast Guard, but her father feared that Liv would
probably not be found until it was light. If she were alive.
Still, he would not let them give up.

For several days after her hospital stay, he was careful
with her, almost in awe, as if he could not believe what had
happened. He continued to blame himself, stewing in the
dark juices of angry guilt for weeks. "If only I'd checked
the filter in the carburetor," he said repeatedly, "none of it
would have happened."

Then it became a lesson, and not just for himself. If Liv
or Sam let something go, anything, from replacing the cap

on the toothpaste to leaving a dish unwashed, he was on them like a pesky horsefly. But there were other lessons as well, ones he couldn't talk about because he didn't know how; ones she couldn't put into words either, because they were so new.

Her father changed. Not all at once, and not a whole lot, but she could tell that he was trying. The way Liv explained it to Spinuchi was that her father was "cracking a little around the edges."

There were lots of little surprises: her father actually asking Liv and Sam what they wanted to watch on the TV; his discovery of popcorn, then caramel corn, which he made himself and made a fuss out of making; coffee beans imported from exotic places (*"I'll bet you haven't tried this one, Liv! And you think you know about coffee"*). He introduced himself to all Liv's teachers on Back-to-School night and told them she was probably too smart for high school. He went to her track meets whenever he could, though she sometimes had to wake him up at the end.

One day he announced that he and Liv would be moving to Santa Barbara. He said the house would need work but it was near the high school. Liv "wouldn't need to bum rides from Spinuchi anymore." It was another of his jokes, the kind he liked best because nobody could ever be sure he was joking.

Then came the biggest surprise of all. It happened one ordinary evening after Liv made a meatloaf so awful it could have been used for a doorstop. Liv's father grabbed her arm so hard, she yelped. Then he cleared his throat several times, frowned across the table at Sam, and said, "Will you marry us?" (After all, he said, they were family. It wasn't only up to him.)

But, mostly, he was his old self. He picked his shells in silence, complained about the weather, the fish cops, the otters. Everything but the sharks; those he seemed to accept as just part of the job.

In the months after the accident there were other fears that turned what happened that day at sea into just a good old story. Sam underwent chemotherapy, losing her curls by the handful until she was bald as a beach ball. For the wedding, she wore a beaded white scarf, a white lace dress from the thrift store, and a smile that lit up the chapel. It was the beginning of waiting, and they did it the way people wait for things they can't stand to wait for: imperfectly, but with courage.

Sam kept her old green Volvo. A new car would never understand her, she said.

The new boat is an old boat with a long pedigree—once the *Judy C*, the *Marni Lee*, the *Mary Ellen*, and finally *Lisa's Hope*, it is now the *Olivia Jean*. It isn't a Radon, it isn't fast or sleek as the *Jeannie T*, but it is all the divers and fishermen could afford. It pleased them to be able to do some payback.

On the shelf over Liv's bed, next to the picture of Gran, the shell from Spinuchi's first legal abalone, the photo of her and Spinuchi at the prom, is the blue cooler lid. It's just a chunk of Styrofoam, her father says. Liv saved herself, he insists, using her wits—"just like her old man."

For Liv's sixteenth birthday her father presented her with a set of sixteen nested abalone shells. Perfect shells, the shells that he had picked clean, night after night, sitting in his old brown chair.